# THE ENGLISH DRAGON BOOK 1

# KATHI S. BARTON

This is a work of fiction. Names, characters, places, and incidents are products of the author's imagination or are used fictitiously and are not to be construed as real. Any resemblance to actual events, locations, organizations, or persons, living or dead, is entirely coincidental.

**World Castle Publishing, LLC**
Pensacola, Florida
Copyright © Kathi S. Barton 2016
Paperback ISBN: 9781629894874
eBook ISBN: 9781629894881
First Edition World Castle Publishing, LLC, June 13, 2016
http://www.worldcastlepublishing.com

**Licensing Notes**

Cover: Karen Fuller
Editor: Eric Johnston
Editor: Maxine Bringenberg

# Chapter 1

Danburn moved to the side of the large lake and stripped off his boots. It wasn't necessary for him to take his clothing off, but he wanted to just sit in the grass for a few minutes before he headed home. He looked over at the large castle and smiled. *Some home*, he thought. It was bigger than the hotel he'd just left a few days ago.

He stood at the very edge of the water and calmed his inner beast. He was hungry for some time of his own, and Danburn had been promising it to him for weeks now. It would give him what he wanted, or Danburn would suffer at his hands. It wouldn't be painful, not really, but it would be annoying. And home was the only place that Danburn could give him the freedom that they both so craved.

Diving into the water, he felt his beast take him. Not all at once, but enough to know that his beast was just as anxious as he was to be free. Parallel with the water, he felt him take all of him, and as soon as he hit the water, there was nothing left of the man he had been.

The water was deeper than it looked. Much like the castle, there were hidden coves and outlets in this lake that no one except a few that he trusted knew about. Danburn swam the distance of the entire lake before flipping and making his way back to swim beneath the earth into the deepest part of it.

Swimming like this wasn't the same as flying, but it was close. The beast, a dragon, was much larger than Danburn by nearly ten times, and weighed several tons. His wings alone were as wide as several football fields laid end to end, and his tail was nearly fifty feet long, covered in thick spikes and dark scales. Danburn had never understood the dynamics of what he was and what he could become, but he did enjoy the way it made him feel.

He was in need of some air several hours later, and slowly rose his snout to the surface of the water to take a breath. As he was breathing in the oxygen, he caught a scent that startled him. Fresh blood. And a great deal of it. Moving to the reeds behind him, Danburn lifted his big head out of the water to look around, knowing that he would be well camouflaged if anyone were to look in his direction. There was not a measure of sound, not a ripple of movement, on the water or around him.

The scent was stronger now, but he could see nothing out of the ordinary. He continued to search just to make sure that nothing was going to come back and bite him in the ass later. It was, after all, his property, and usually everyone knew better than to trespass on his land. As he watched, something moved at the corner of his vision. It was then that he saw what his nose had already told him.

The woman was making her way to the water, slowly

looking around as much as he was for something to come upon her. He could see that she was hurt. The blood stained the water even as she made her way to the deeper part, which was several hundred yards from where he was. Danburn looked around again when she ducked under the water, knowing that she'd not be able to stay under long because of her being human. He could taste it in the scent of her blood as she hid below the surface.

A man—or now that he could see them, men—were walking to where she was. Danburn didn't want to interfere, especially in his current form, so he waited. When one of the men lifted a rifle, pointing it in the direction the woman had gone, Danburn dipped beneath the water just as the shot was fired.

When he saw her, it appeared she'd been hit. Her eyes were closed, not in death, but in pain. Blood pooled around them both as he reached her. Grabbing her gently with his clawed hand, he pulled her body to his and swam to the underground tunnel of his home. He knew that someone would be there. His friend and go-to man, Noah, would be there if no one else was. Emerging from the water, he handed the limp woman to Noah and dove back into the waters without a word. He had to make sure that she was safe, whoever she was, as well as his home.

Two of the four men were in the water when he emerged from the reeds. Danburn didn't even bother trying to figure out what they were doing there, or even what they had wanted the woman for, but pulled them both under the water and held them there until they no longer struggled. When he was satisfied that they were no longer a threat, he moved to the surface again and waited for someone, either man, to come into the water to retrieve the now floating bodies of their comrades.

They were being very cautious, but he was a very patient man and could wait them out for hours. Just as one of the men moved to the edge of the water, he heard the sounds of the sirens coming. Noah, he thought, had called someone for him. As the men scrambled away, leaving the dead for him to deal with, Danburn sank beneath the surface again and headed back to the cove where he'd taken the woman.

Noah was there, as was his personal physician, Pierce Cunningham. Noah said nothing as he held out a towel for him when he shifted to his body and climbed out of the water, shaking a few of his scales into the depths to replenish what he'd done to it. Leaving the dead behind would harm the lake only a little, but he hated doing it. Noah fussed at him then, telling him he should have taken better care. Noah was sometimes worse than his mother could be when it came to him.

"I couldn't let her die, you know." Nothing but a small huff of a sound. As he took the towel and dried his legs, he was handed a shirt and tie. "We have a guest?"

"Yes. A party. In your mother's honor. I'm not sure what we're to do with this injured woman, but I'm just glad that we have no guests coming. I don't think it would bode well for you if anyone found out." Danburn paused in getting dressed and looked at the woman, then back at Noah. "Pierce is doing the best he can with her. The beating she took was bad, but Pierce said that with a little rest she'll be good as new. The gunshot wounds, however, will need some tending to."

"Wounds? As in more than one?" Noah told him there were two total on her person. "I only heard the one shot. I had no idea that...by the way, there are two bodies in the lake. They drowned."

Noah tisked at him, and Danburn had to hide a smile. The man was such a prude. As he pulled on his pants, not bothering with the underwear held out for him, he asked Noah what the police were called for.

"I've no idea, my lord." He was in trouble if Noah was calling him *lord*. "Perhaps they heard of a large dragon swimming in the waterways and drowning people, and someone took it upon themselves to call the law. Or perhaps they think that having a shot up woman in their realm is something else that they might fumble into, and half blindly find the culprit."

"You're in a mood, aren't you?" Noah snatched the towel from him and walked away. "I'm fine, in the event you were going to ask. No shots to my poor body."

"We should be so lucky, my lord."

Danburn was still laughing as he made his way to the upper levels. He made sure that the woman was cared for and put into one of the many bedrooms, but out of sight of the household. He had no idea who she was, but no one physically hurt women—and that was all there was to it.

When he entered the living room, his mother stood up and came to him.

"You smell of lake water." He kissed her on the cheek and told her she smelled wonderful. "Good save, but it does not negate that while I was here wasting away, waiting for you to come and wish me a happy birthday, you were having a nice dip in the water. Danburn, you know I hate it when you're late."

"I know, Mom, but this couldn't be helped." He told her what he'd come upon, and she wanted to see the woman right away. "Pierce is working with her. He's to come and get me if there are any problems with her when she wakes. He said she took a hell of a beating."

"You didn't really kill those men, did you? Right on your own lake?" He told her that there was little choice in that too. "I'm sure that once their bodies are found there will be questions. Do you know who the other two were?"

"No, but I know what they look like and what they smell like." Dinner was announced, and he escorted her into the dining room. There would be cake later, after her favorite meal of lobster and steak, then he'd give her his gifts. He might have forgotten about what the date was, but he never forgot her birthday.

Dinner was a quiet affair with just the two of them. He did try to get Noah to come and have cake with them, but he only glared, something that he was quite good at, and told them that he'd have some later, with the rest of the staff.

No one could put themselves in a class better than Noah did. The man was pompous as well as correct, but Danburn loved him with all of his heart. And he was pretty sure that Noah loved him as well. The two of them had been together for as long as Danburn had been alive, and that had been a long time.

"I've been thinking of taking a trip." He didn't mention that he had the same idea for her in the form of a cruise, but only nodded at his mom's statement. "With you closing up the house here, I just don't think I can stand to be around to see it. We've been here for so long, Danburn, that I don't know what I'll do without being able to come here."

"I'm closing the house, not tearing it down. And I've told you several times, you can live here for as long as you want. I just need to be closer to my work." She nodded, but he could see the sadness there. "Mom, what is it really? Is it Dad? Do you not want to leave him?"

He knew that his mom went to talk to his dad daily. He'd died some two hundred years ago when he'd let an infection get into one of his wings and it had spread to his heart before they could do anything about it. Even as immortals there were things that could kill them, and poisoning of the blood was the biggest one.

"I can talk to him anywhere, but yes, that's part of it." She sat down before the blazing fire and looked at it instead of him as she continued. "I love this place. I understand that you need to be closer to your job and all. But this is home to me. And to you. I wish…there are times when I wish I had taken my own home instead of coming here to yours. I should have thought that if you found a mate, she'd want to run her own home and not have me around."

"Don't say that, Mom. Please don't. I'm not going to have a mate this late in my life. And even if I do, if she doesn't like you, there is no way I'm going to love her. I'm not going to sell this place or leave it to ruin. I just think it'll be better in the long run for me to settle elsewhere. At least for the time being." He didn't tell her the real reason, but he had a feeling that she knew. The house was lonely without his dad there. He'd been a rock in his otherwise turbulent life. "Why don't you let me give you my gifts? I know that you've been trying to get information from Noah."

"Yes. And he's as stubborn as you are." After winking at her, he went to get the boxes. There were several of them; he would find things for her throughout the year and send them here to give to her for this occasion. "Oh, so many. Danburn, you spoil me rotten, you know that, don't you?"

"Yes, but you make it so easy." She hugged him to her, longer and tighter than normal, and he pulled her to him when she started to back away. "I love you, Mom. And will forever."

Long after she went up to bed, he sat in the den watching the fire. He'd been to check on the woman, and there was no change in her. He'd also asked Noah to find out where the police were going, and so far there was nothing on that either. Only that they'd gone to the property near him, the one where he knew the new owner was up to no good. Not until someone knocked on the front door did he realize how late it had become. Or that it had started raining.

~~~

Kendrick felt like a drowned rat. Her hair was plastered to her head, and her coat was as soaked clear through. The boots she had on, usually made for this sort of weather, had gotten a leak in them a few days ago, and she'd thought for sure she'd be able to afford a new pair by now. Then her sister.... *Well, it is always Louisa, now isn't it?* Kendrick thought. One thing or another was always befalling her sister. Reaching for the giant knocker on the door again, she nearly screamed when a man suddenly opened the door and stared at her.

"I was wondering if I could use your phone." He stood there so still she wondered for a moment if he was real. "I broke down a few miles back, and I dropped my phone in a puddle and it no longer works."

*Lie,* she told herself as her face heated up at the fib. The phone didn't work because Louisa had stolen her money for the bill and it had gone dead for lack of payment. Like her boots and her now overdue rent, there was no money to take care of even the simplest things, including food. Louisa was going to ruin her more than she already had.

As the man continued to stare at her, she had the most overwhelming urge to snap her fingers in front of him to see if he was sleepwalking.

"Or not. I guess we can just stand here, staring at each other until one of us dies from the cold and wet. I'm thinking it'll be me, since you're all snug as a bug in the house." He still did nothing. "Christ. Is there someone here that speaks? Any language? I know a few that we can try out."

"The master of the house has gone to bed." Well, big fucking deal. She didn't want the master of anything, just a fucking phone. "If you were to wait here, I'll retrieve the phone for you and you may use it."

The door closed so fast that she had no time to tell him to forget it. She stood there for several seconds, wondering why she was even bothering about this, then turned and made her way back to the driveway. Fuck this shit. Louisa was on her own.

Three hours ago, Louisa had called her and told her that she was in trouble, which by Kendrick's estimation happened about four times a day. It was out of the pan and into the fire for her sister. Just trying to figure out how she did it was usually more of an effort than she cared to make any more. But the call had come, and she'd driven her piece of shit car to where Louisa said she was, to bail her out if she could. There was no money, so if that was going to be it, Louisa was going to have to deal with it on her own. But who the fuck knew there really was an English castle here?

The night was so nasty and cold that she wished now that she'd stayed home. No matter what she did for Louisa, it was never enough, nor did it keep her out of the next bout of trouble. But when she'd mentioned guns and men, like an idiot, Kendrick had dropped everything to come to her rescue. And more than likely had lost yet another job because she couldn't stay until the end of her shift. Life with her sister was as bad is it came, she thought.

"I should have my head examined. Again." She huddled into her soaking wet coat and stomped her way back to the main road to her broken down car. "Come and get me, she said. They have guns and they're going to kill me. Perhaps I'd get some peace and quiet if they did."

Stopping in her tracks, Kendrick felt herself start to cry at what she'd said. There was no way she'd leave Louisa to get shot just so she'd leave her alone. She loved her sister more than she did herself at times. But it was becoming too much. She was broke, thanks to her, late on all her bills, again thanks to her sister, and she'd not had a decent meal in longer than she could remember. Her belly seconded that comment by growling loudly.

Louisa was a good person when she wanted to be...mostly when she needed something or someone to do something for her. Her troubles, Kendrick knew, happened because she was so demanding, and when someone told her that she was going to get this or that for her troubles, she believed them. Kendrick had learned her lessons at the hand of a very nasty person, namely her own mother, and knew that trusting anyone could get you killed. Or worse.

"Beat me once, shame on you. Beat me a couple of dozen more times, and I have to learn to run and hide better." She stood in the middle of the field, not having a clue where she was, and then heard a sound behind her. "Fuck."

Diving into the brush closest to her, she lay as still as she could, trying not to think about what might be sharing the place with her as two men walked by her. One of them, she knew, was the quiet man at the door.

"I was bringing her the phone. Why would she leave when I told her that I would bring her the phone?" The other man said nothing but grunted. "It's not my fault that she has not the sense of a toad to get in out of the rain. I guess I could have talked to her more, but I was so shocked to see her there that I was rendered speechless for too long." She wanted to get up and tell him had he invited her in, she'd not have been in the rain, but said nothing.

The two of them were just passing her when they stopped suddenly. Sure that they'd found her, she wished now that she'd brought some sort of weapon with her. A rock would have made her feel better than she did at the moment.

"She's here. I can smell her." The other man lifted his nose to the air, and Kendrick had a feeling that he really could smell her. She'd left work so quickly to get to Louisa that she'd not had time to change her clothing. She knew she smelled of french fries and greasy meat. "You look over there and I'll go this way. And for Christ's sake, Noah, don't step on her. Danburn is pissed enough about this."

"Yes. I will try. She didn't appear to be injured. But I will be careful." The other man—Sniffer, she decided to call him— told him to hush. As Sniffer made his way toward her, she closed her eyes and wished she was home in her own bed, wished it as hard as she'd wished for a great many things lately.

Peeking beneath her lashes, she knew that someone was standing over her. She saw his boots first. And the insane thought of how expensive they looked and how totally out of her league they were was running through her mind when he bent his knee to become eye level with her. He didn't say anything but put out his hand to her, which she refused to take.

"I just wanted to call someone. I don't know who it might have been, but I thought someone could help me out." He said nothing but kept his hand where it was. "Why don't you pretend that you didn't find me? I'll go back to my car and sit there until either this monsoon takes me away or the sun comes up. I'm sure this Danburn person wouldn't care a fig if you just left me here."

"It won't work. He's very stubborn. And until one of us shows up with you, my boss will make us keep looking for you. He is, at this moment, looking in the opposite direction that you took, by the way. Did you know that you are about five feet from the lake?" She didn't even bother turning. It would be her luck that it was just a ploy to catch her off guard…or maybe there really was a lake behind her. One with a great big monster in it. "There is one. It's deeper than it looks, and holds all sorts of secrets that you are better off not knowing."

"Right now I wouldn't care if something lurking it in came out and gobbled me up. I'm so fucked right now." He nodded, but said nothing more. "I don't suppose you know a woman by the name of Louisa Barrera, do you? She's my sister, and the reason I'm out here this late at night." He told her that he did not. "Well, it was worth a shot."

Standing up on her own, she watched the man as he put two fingers into his mouth and made the most amazing sound she'd ever heard. Being called a simple whistle wasn't enough. It was perfectly pitched and loud enough to wake the dead. The man from the doorway came toward them with a small flashlight. It occurred to her then that she had one in her glove box, but the battery was more than likely dead. Why should that work out for her?

"You should have waited, miss. I was returning with the phone." She wanted to say something along the lines of she hadn't felt welcome, but didn't. "The master of the house is most upset with you. He said he has enough going on right now, and he's right. Danburn is usually right."

"Me? Why is he upset with me? I didn't do anything but ask to use the phone. You guys came out in the rain to find me. And I doubt very much he's always right. Bossy more than likely, but not always right." She was sloshing back with them in the event that one of them would offer to give her a lift back to her car, which she'd only just realized was in the opposite direction from where they were headed. "I think we're going the wrong way. I just want to go home now. I'll find her in the morning. Why I believed her when she said that men with guns were after her, I have no idea."

"Guns? Your sister told you there were men with guns after her? Well, if that's the case, I think we might know her after all." She stopped moving when Sniffer spoke. She was still standing there when he turned and looked at her. "Blonde with dark eyes. A mark on her left arm that looks like someone touched it with a curling iron?"

"I have no idea what color her hair is now. It's been a couple of days since I've actually.... Never mind. The mark, it was a branding iron. One of her boyfriends thought it would be cool if they branded each other. She was first, and he chickened out when she screamed and fainted. Where is she? Dead? Please tell me she's all right." He assured her that when he'd left to find her she was fine. "I can take her now if you'll just let me use the phone to call in a favor. My car won't...it's too far for me to take her back by walking."

"She's been shot." Kendrick felt her knees just give out, and something—or she supposed some*one*—scooped her up before she fell. The voice of the man, strong and angry, made her struggle against him, but he commanded her to be still and she did.

"What were you thinking walking around in the rain like a fool? You could have been killed or drowned. Do you have

17

the sense that God gave you?" She struggled again and he told her to be still. "If you fall now, I will simply have Noah get the car and run you over several times for scaring the household."

"You are a charmer, aren't you? I bet all the women around just fall at your feet from the way nice things just roll off your forked tongue. Let me go, you buffoon. I just want to get my sister and get the hell away from you people." He laughed, and Kendrick wanted to hit him, but they were suddenly standing in the hallway of the most beautiful area she'd ever been in. "Where the hell am I? Dead?"

"No, you are not dead. There is something decidedly wrong with you, isn't there?" She looked at him then, really looked, and wished to Christ she hadn't. Men like him, handsome and sexy, were not something one like her saw much of. If ever. "This is my home. And you are an unwelcome intruder. Had you not upset my household, I would be sleeping in my bed, not soaked to the skin looking for you in the rain."

"Danburn!" The woman's voice coming from the staircase sounded shocked. It took all the energy Kendrick had to tear her eyes away from the hunk of nasty beauty to look at her. "*Nous ne traitons pas invité cette façon. Quel est ton problème?*"

"I'm not a guest, but an intruder, as he called me. And if you're going to speak a different language to chew him out, you should know that I can speak more than most people." Kendrick looked at the man, then back at the woman. "As for what is wrong with him. I would say that he's not any different than he normally is, a nasty dispositioned prick that got up on the wrong side of the bed today, and is taking it out on the people around him like it's his job. Like he does daily."

The woman laughed and reached out her hand. "Hello, my dear. I'm the nasty dispositioned prick's mother, Lady English. I'm to understand from Noah that your sister is here.

Let me take you to her."

As they moved by the big man, Kendrick couldn't help herself. She stuck her tongue out at him and flipped him off. There was going to be hell to pay for that, she was sure, but right now she felt like she'd won a small battle. And she had a feeling that there were going to be a few more battles before this was done.

# Chapter 2

"You have seven meetings today, three of them before lunch. A meeting with Mrs. James at eleven-thirty, and then..."

"Where is she?" Noah asked him who. "That woman. The sister to the one that I brought here. Where is she sleeping? Has she been fed and given clean clothing?"

"To my knowledge, she is still with her sister and has been most of the night. Mary said that she'd not left her but to use the bathroom and to inquire about something to drink for herself. She did come down for some toast about four this morning. And we would not allow anyone to sit around in wet things in the house, sir. No matter what has brought them to us." Danburn had started for the offices that Pierce, his physician, worked from when Noah stopped him. He knew the man was upset with him. But damn it, there were strangers in the house. "My lord, she was moved to a room. The pink one on the second floor, sir."

He started for the stairs, wondering what he'd done now.

A "my lord" and a "sir" all in one statement meant that he'd done something terrible. He'd deal with it later. Danburn took the stairs two at a time to get this taken care of. What he didn't expect when he opened the door after a brief knock was to find the woman from last night crying.

"What is wrong with you?" She told him it was none of his business. "Of course it is. You're in my home, using my things. Everything you do here is my business. Answer me right now. I want you to go down and get something to eat, too. There is no point in you getting ill and having to prolong your stay."

"How much money do you have? Do you own a car? Or do you have a limo service cart your ass all over the place?" Danburn felt his anger burn at him, and told her that it was none of her concern. "So you can keep your own business matters private, but no one else can? I guess I should have expected that from a man like you. Don't you think that's a little one sided? And I'll eat when I want, what I want. As soon as Louisa is able to move, we'll be out of your hair anyway."

"I don't care for your tone. Most people do what I tell them without hesitation. I don't care for you telling me what you will do." She looked at Noah when he walked in with Mary, who was carrying a small tray. Before Danburn could guess her intent, the woman got up, thanked Mary, and took the tray from her. "What do you think you're doing?"

"Helping her. Us domestics have to stick together, I think. As for people doing what you tell them, I'm pretty sure that my sister and I are the only ones not on your payroll, so of course they do what you tell them." She set down the tray that he only just noticed had tea and a bottle of over the counter pain reliever on it. He turned to Noah when he laughed. "Ah, you don't care for that either."

"Care for what?" She told him laughter. "Of course I do. Just not at my expense." As she struggled to open the bottle, he reached out and took it from her to open it. She snatched it right back and glared at him.

"You are the rudest man I've ever had the displeasure of meeting. Don't you have old women to throw out on their collective asses or something?" He took a step back from her and she glared harder. "You do that? You throw people out of their homes? I should have guessed it earlier from your mean disposition and lack of good manners. Your mother must be very ashamed of you."

"I most certainly do not have bad manners. I am this way because I've had my sleep taken from me by having to look out for someone without enough sense to come in out of the rain. And what I do is called foreclosure. Had they made the payments on time, there would be no reason to toss them out on their collective asses, as you so delicately put it." He wasn't sure what he expected her to do next, but when she turned her back to him and sobbed, he took a step toward her. As soon as he put his hand on her shoulder to...he supposed comfort her, she turned and slapped him on the cheek. "What, pray tell, was that for?"

"I want you to leave us alone." He took a step back from her. The anger in her body and voice was palpable. "Get out. You heard me, get out of here."

He was nearly to work when he touched the place where she had hit him. It wasn't sore — she wasn't able to hurt him, not a mere human — but it did sting in a way that made him regret not just allowing her to do it, but forcing her hand in doing so. Not that he had any idea what he'd done to provoke such a response, but she had hit him.

"Do you know anything about her?" Noah said that he

had someone working on it. "Tell me what you find out. You do know that whatever those men wanted of her sister, they're not going to stop at just hurting her."

"Pierce mentioned that the sister smelled of fast food, probably a burgers and fries sort of establishment. I'm going to see if I can get Connie to get some information from her today." Danburn nodded. Connie Weeks was his secretary, and she could dig out the most useful information when he needed her to. "The younger woman is most unusual, is she not? I mean, she dislikes you, but there is a quality about her that makes the staff want to protect her."

"She's violent too. Why did she hit me? I didn't do anything that warranted such a response from her." Noah said nothing, but Danburn saw the ghost of a smile. He wanted to ask him what it meant, but thought he'd be better off not knowing. "Make sure that there are extra guards around the house until the two of them are gone. And tell Mom that I'd prefer that she stayed away from her. We know nothing about either of them, and I want to keep it that way."

By the time Noah dropped him off at his offices, they had gone over his schedule again. The meetings wouldn't be too bad, not the ones before lunch anyway. He did have that thing with Julia that he had been looking forward to getting over with, but now he wasn't so sure.

Julia James was in trouble. Trouble that she'd brought on herself, but he wasn't going to be sucked into it as she had planned. Now he was glad that he'd made a few inquiries a month ago and backed off. Julia didn't know it as yet, but she and her brother were in some serious shit, and he was going to help bring her down.

Danburn had been approached by the Federal Bureau of Investigation just after he'd put in a few calls about Julia and her brother. The Feds had filled him in on a great many things, one of them being that her brother had committed all kinds of acts that were going to earn him some very serious prison time. And Julia was just as deep in it as he was.

Had it been up to Danburn, he would have broken things off with her weeks ago. Not that it mattered. Until the government men had approached him, he'd only been using her for a sexual partner, and she'd been someone to hang on his arm when he needed a date. But now it was about to come to a head, and he was going to celebrate when it was done. Today was going to be a good day, he hoped.

At nine-thirty he looked up when his door opened. He had no idea who he expected to be there, but it certainly wasn't Noah. Not yet at any rate. Standing up, reaching for his jacket as he waited for him to speak, Danburn knew that something had happened to his mom. Those women had hurt her, he knew it.

"They're gone." He asked Noah who. "The women. They made a call just after you left, and then someone in a very old van took them away, your mother told me. Louisa was in a great deal of pain, but Pierce gave her something for it. Their names are Louisa and Kendrick Barrera, by the way. When I returned home this morning, I spoke to your mother and finished the list that you gave me before I went to talk to Mary. She was cleaning the room when I went to check on the two of them."

Noah sat down, something he'd never done before in his presence. Danburn sat in the chair across the couch from him and waited for him to speak. He was afraid, and Danburn was seldom afraid of anything. But something had upset Noah, and he didn't care for feeling so helpless.

"Noah, what happened? I mean, it's not like you to come

back here to tell me that they left. What else happened there at the house?" Noah looked at him, and he could see the pain in his eyes. "Did they hurt you? Or anyone at home?"

"Not that I've been made aware of. But I never saw them...the Barrera sisters, I mean. The two men from a van came into the house, Mary told me, gathered up Louisa, and then they all left with Kendrick. There were no harsh words. In fact, Mary said that other than thanking her for helping, Kendrick said nothing at all. I spoke with your mother and she was most upset with you." Danburn nodded. Of course, Kendrick had probably blamed him for all of this. "She seems to think that you should have done more to help her."

"I have no idea what that might have been. It's not like I caused her sister to be hurt. And I didn't tell them they had to leave right now. But they're gone now, so that's all that matters." Noah shook his head. "What else was I supposed to do? Give them keys to the vault in the basement? Let them live there for the rest of their lives while we sat back and let them rob us blind? I swear to Christ, you try to do a good thing and it comes back to bite you in the ass."

"Mistress wants me to find them. She told me that she would...well, she can be most persuasive when she needs to be. But I am to find them for her, and find out if they are in need of anything." Noah looked at him. "I wouldn't even know where to begin in telling her what they need. They don't have much at all. When I was looking into things, as you asked me to do, I found that while Kendrick does work, she is behind in all of her bills."

"I don't understand why Mother would even care." Noah said he didn't understand women at all, so he could not help him there. "You found them, I take it. I'm assuming that they don't live in the lap of luxury? You do know that this entire thing is more than likely a scam, right? That they found out that I'm closing up the castle and moving here, and in a few weeks they'll say they left something behind and will get into the house. The next thing we know, they're living there and there isn't shit we can do about it."

Noah said nothing, but the longer he sat there, Danburn could see the anger surfacing on his face. Even his body was stiff with it. Good, that meant that they'd not get by anyone at his home while he was away. Noah would take—

"I shall leave you now, sir. I'm not sure why I even came by." He stood up and so did Danburn. There was a stiffness there that Danburn was sort of leery of. "When will you be returning home this evening? I shall have Mary leave you a plate should it be too late."

"What the hell just happened here?" Noah told him he had no idea what he meant. "You're angry. And the reason I know that is because you look like someone stuck a pole up your ass, and you're calling me sir again. You know how I hate that."

"Yes, I do." As Noah made his way to the door, Danburn felt lost and pissed. But he wasn't sure why he should be feeling either emotion. "I shall see you this evening, sir."

After he was gone, Danburn wanted to throw something. He didn't care what it was or even what it might break when he did, but he was pissed enough that he wanted to destroy something. It was a feeling that seemed to overwhelm him a great deal lately, and he hated it.

Going to his desk, he did a search on the two women and found nothing other than an obit stating that they were the only living children of their mother, Nettie Barrera. And searching for her name, he found several articles mentioning her being a wanted woman in the attempted murder of a minor.

His frustration grew when he found an article dated several months ago about Louisa. She'd been arrested and released on bail when the people she'd been with were caught up in a robbery. Nothing more was mentioned about her involvement, nor about why she'd not gone to jail. Danburn called his friend at the police station, Jake Ludlow.

"Yeah, I know them both. Mostly the older of the two. Louisa has a history, I'll tell you that much. As for the sister, the only time we see her is when she comes in to bail Louisa out. Not for anything major like the other one." Danburn asked him what sort of stuff. "Parking violation once. Some trouble with a neighbor about trashcans not being taken back when they were empty. Stupid shit like that. Kendrick is a good kid that has been dealt a bad hand. I'll tell you about it when I see you next time if you're interested. Her sister, Louisa, is a piece of work that makes me think that she's always going to be in trouble somehow. She isn't bad, but seems to find herself in situations that go bad. And she's very…well, gullible, if you want to know the truth. I think she needs a keeper. But yeah, I can send you over what I have on her."

"Do you know anything about Kendrick? I mean, other than she bails her sister out? And has shitty neighbors?" There was silence on the other end, and he was sure that Jake was going to tell him it was none of his business. He was getting sick of hearing that. "Jake? What is it?"

"Kendrick is on our radar, but not like you think. Hang on." He heard the sounds behind the man suddenly cut out. "She's a good girl, like I said. Works hard. But with a sister like hers, she runs into trouble too, and gets hurt when she feels the need to tread where we'd think twice about going. But because of Louisa, Kendrick is behind in her rent, bills going unpaid. Twice recently she's had run-ins with her landlord. Mostly, I think, he's pissy because she's not sleeping with him, but she is behind in a lot of things. In fact, in two days I have to go and evict her. She knows about it. I already talked to her last week and gave her a little extra time so she could see if she could get the money. But she told me that she's already working her ass off at four jobs and can't swing it. I think Louisa is draining her."

"You mean financially." Jake told him it was more than that. Like she literally was draining her by sucking her dry of life. "I see."

"Like I keep saying, Kendrick is a really good girl. Polite to a fault. Never gets herself into trouble on her own, and the only time I saw her lose her temper was when Louisa wouldn't see reason." Jake laughed. "That's something you should be made aware of. Louisa has this thing about her. She's very set in what she wants, and will drive you to want to hit her until you just give in. I think that's what happens with Kendrick. She just can't fight against her anymore."

"So I have these two women that my mom is looking for. One has been hurt, the other will be homeless soon. Do you know if they live together?" Jake said he didn't know if Louisa had her own address or not, but he'd been told to use Kendrick's. "You think they're scamming you, and me eventually?"

"No. I really don't. Kendrick might be blinded by her sister, but she's far from stupid. She told me once she can speak ten languages. I've actually used her a couple of times when I had someone that I didn't understand. She works hard and pays you back when she can." Jake laughed again. "Louisa, however? I'd not trust her with money as far as I could throw her. I'd not lend her anything unless you never want to see it again. And if she wants something from you, walk away.

She'll make you nuts to have you see it her way."

Danburn wasn't sure he'd trust either one of them, but Jake had always been honest with him, and he didn't doubt that he might feel this way about the two of them. His mom would have to leave them alone. He didn't want any more trouble coming his way right now.

"By the way, those two men that we found in your lake. Do you know anything about them, other than that they're dead? And you do know that they're not the sort that goes hunting, right? Both of them were armed like they were going to war, but no ID, wallet, or even a cell that we could look at. Anything you can tell me about that?" Jake laughed. "I have a feeling that somehow, with you asking about her, Louisa is involved in this, and Kendrick might be as well."

He knew he could trust the man. But did he trust him enough to let him know everything about the two men? He'd find out. Danburn knew that as well, so he told him what he knew. Not that he'd drowned the men, but that they'd turned up on his land and that Louisa had been shot.

"Christ love a duck. All right. But this is between the two of us." Danburn told him of course. "The two men work for a man by the name of Bernie Bullock. I think you might have heard of him."

"The guy who a few years ago started buying up land around the area and close to my land. And from what I've read in the papers, about six or seven months ago he moved in. Yeah, so?" Jake told him there was more to it, and that he thought the man was up to no good. "I think I might have tried to tell you that when you guys came out to tell me he was using the land with a government grant. And weren't there some rules he was supposed to abide by? I'm guessing that he's not, if they're armed like you said these two were."

"There were rules. And no, I don't think he is. But he made some sort of deal with the big guys in office. Leasing the property for ninety-nine years, then it reverts back to the state. He has guidelines, like you said, that he has to meet and all, but they don't have it in their budget to enforce these rules. So he pretty much does what he wants out there unless we have to be called in. Twice now we've been summoned out there for someone dying. And that's only been in the last six weeks." Danburn asked him what had happened. "What we're being told—and the bodies do have the appearance of it—is that they hanged themselves. Too far from their families or something like that."

"And this has to do with the Barrera sisters, how?" Jake told him he didn't know as yet, but he'd bet anything that Louisa did. "Christ. They were both at my house. I wonder what sort of shit that is going to cause me."

"Hang on." When he was put on hold, Danburn started making a list of things he had to do to keep himself out of the middle of their drama. And he had no doubt there was a lot of it with these two. When Jake came back on the line, he sounded upset. "Danburn, if you want to just happen to drive by her apartment, you might see for yourself what kind of shit this girl is in."

He wrote down the address and grabbed his jacket again. As he was telling his secretary he'd be back soon, she asked him about his appointments. Danburn did something he'd never done before. He told her to clear his day. She was as shocked about it as he was. And Connie Weeks was not one to shock easily.

~~~

Kendrick wanted to cry, stomp her foot, and simply burst into tears and have a hissy fit. But it wouldn't solve anything, and she'd still be trying to figure out how to get out of this mess. Again.

"I'm real sorry, Kendrick." She waved the man off. He'd been by her house five times over the last few months, collecting on her electric bill so she'd not have it turned off. But today there had been no money to pay him with. She didn't even have the money to make a call had there been anyone she could have called. "I've called the cops. You know that they gotta be involved too. Especially since he wants you out right now."

"Yes. I know. Mr. Dickface is having a cow." He laughed and stood with her while they waited on the police. "I really don't blame him for being mad at me. I would be too if he was behind in his rent for three months. I've tried so hard, Peter. I'm so tired of this."

Peter told her again how sorry he was. She knew he was. He was the nicest collector she'd ever had to deal with. Once, when she was ten dollars short of paying the least amount she had to pay, he'd chipped in to help her out.

Her coat from last night was still soaking wet, so all she had to wear was her tattered sweater. Her shoes were wet too, from walking around for hours to find Louisa. So now she was standing in the cold with only a ratty sweater to keep her warm, and shoes that were so worn that she was surprised that they even stayed on her feet. Peter was dressed in heavy wool pants, a jacket that looked warm enough to keep her heated all winter, and boots that were so shiny that she'd bet he put something on them every time he got into his car to keep them looking so good. But the man had been nothing but nice to her since she moved here several months ago.

"Peter, you want something to drink? I have some tea brewing. It's not that fancy stuff we serve at the restaurant, but I can fix you some."

"No thanks, hun. I'm just sorry this has to happen now." She wanted to tell him it was never a good time to have your power shut off, but there was little she could do now.

Louisa was asleep in her bed and resting well, thanks to the drugs that the nice doctor at the house had given her. For now, anyway. Kendrick, as usual, was dealing with the outcome of one or another of her scraps. She was so fucked right now. When Jake Ludlow showed up, his cruiser pulling up behind Peter's truck, she wanted to beg him to take her to jail. She was sure that she'd eat better and be warmer.

"Miss Barrera." He tipped his hat at her, and she gave him a watery smile. "I understand that we're having some issues here. Do you have a heavier coat? It's cold out here."

"You're damned right we're having issues. She's fucking four months behind in her rent. And now—" Kendrick told Donavan Phillips it was only three months and she was working on that. "Well, that does me little good now, don't it? You're not gonna be able to live there with no power in the place, and I can't rent it with the mess you left it in."

"I can too live here." She looked at Jake, who cleared his throat. "I have to live there, Officer Ludlow. I have nowhere else to go. And my sister is hurt."

"I'm sorry, honey, but he's right. Since we got involved, I can't let you stay where it's not safe." She felt the tears burn her eyes. "Where's Louisa? Is she in there too?"

"Yes. But I can't move her. She was hurt again, and they gave her something to make her sleep. She's in my bed resting." Jake nodded, and she had a feeling he already knew what had happened to her. That damned man, the king of the castle. "Did he call you last night, or early this morning?"

"This morning." She turned her back to them all. It was

33

that or let them see her crying. "Kendrick, I can take you to the shelter. And Louisa should be in the hospital. Why don't you let me help you gather a few things and I'll take you myself?"

"I can't live there and you know it. The last time I was there Louisa got us into trouble, and I'm not allowed to darken their steps again. Or at least I think it was me they were talking to. And there isn't money for a hospital, even if I could get her there." Jake nodded, and she watched a big limo pull up across the street. She knew who it was even before he was let out of the monster thing, and wondered if Jake had called him in so he could have a show. "If you'll call an ambulance please, I'll figure something out. Just don't let that man take over."

"I want my money." So did she, but Donavan wasn't going to be put off any more. Not that he'd been all that helpful before, but now he was in the right and she wasn't. "Right now, Barrera. Pay up."

"You know as well as I do that if I had the money, none of this would be going on. Just sell my things. There's not much there anyway, and I'll get you the rest." When Donavan came at her, she knew that he was going to hit her and tightened up in a sort of ball to take it. And it wouldn't be the first time. But his fist was stayed by the man from the castle.

"Touch her and I will have you so tied up in knots that nothing will untangle you." The threat, because there was no doubt to her that that was what it was, was delivered with a calmness that scared her. And it wasn't even directed at her. "Get over there until I call for you."

"You can't talk to me that way. I run this place. And she's out of favors as far as I'm concerned." Donovan's big beefy hand still covered the man's fist. "Showing off for the bitch, are you? Well, got news for you, she don't put out. Not even for a little rent money."

Kendrick had no idea what she was going to do when she turned to the landlord, but as soon as she did, the pain in the side of her head exploded. Stars even did a little jig as she felt the world tilt at an odd angle and someone began to curse. Kendrick had to smile. She didn't know why she knew it was the man from the castle, but fell forward thinking it was funny to hear him lose his temper, and it not aimed at her. Then she was out.

Moving hurt her head, and something about it made her feel woozy. She was sick too. There were no two ways about it, whatever had happened had affected her belly, and there was a rebellion going on there. As she held her head, ringing started just as she realized that someone was talking to her. Screaming at her really. In a surreal sort of way, she knew that her landlord was laying on the ground beside her.

"Can you hear me?" Nodding made her sicker, so she told the man yes. "What the hell were you doing stepping into my fist like that? Do you have a fucking death wish?"

"Yes, that's it. I have a death wish. I'm pretty sure that any person would have the same sort of feelings when you're around screaming at them like.... You hit me?" It was suddenly too much. Leaning to her side, she threw up. Three times. There was little on her belly since there wasn't any food in the house, but her belly didn't seem to care. When she leaned back to try and lay down, the man yelled again for her to wake up. "I'm not sleeping, you moronic fuck. I hurt."

"You will not pass out on me again." She glared at him as best she could, but he seemed out of focus. "You're going to the hospital. I cannot believe that you made me hit you."

"*I* made you hit *me*? How the hell do you figure that? Just go away. You're not nice. I don't like you, either. You're a bully and a dick." Kendrick thought perhaps someone laughed, but she didn't really care. It was becoming more and more difficult to focus on things, and she was sick again. "Just let me die right here. I don't know what you'll do with my body, as I have no insurance nor the money to be buried with, but I want to just lay down and die."

"You don't have my permission to die." That was the stupidest thing she'd ever heard, and told him that. "You are the most stubborn pain in the ass woman I have ever met. I want you to sit up and look at me so I can tell how badly you were hurt."

"Right back at you, you good looking fuck wad." It was getting to be too much. Her head was coming apart, and she was going to be sick again. Instead of doing as the moron was demanding of her, Kendrick let her body just slip away.

# Chapter 3

"She's pissed off, in the event you weren't aware of that." Danburn nodded. Of course she'd blame him for this too. "I don't think I'm going to allow you to go back and see her. Not today at any rate. Kendrick is barely holding on now, and I don't think seeing you is going to help her any."

"Holding onto what?" Dr. Thomas Bailey, the ER doctor and Danburn's good friend, told him she was trying not to lose it. "I'm sure that she's thinking that's my fault too. Did you hear her cursing me when she came in here? I have never in my life been called those names…I think she was making most of those up."

"I'm sure she was." Tom laughed. "I've seen her in here a couple of times over the last few months. She never tells me who it is that knocks her around, but I would imagine that it's the landlord or that prick of a boss she has. Nice girl. But I didn't have any idea that she could string words together like that. I think you're bringing that out in her. Goes to show you that some people have an inner lioness that they keep hidden away until they're backed into a corner."

Danburn decided to ignore that. Everyone seemed to be blaming him for everything that happened to this woman. Sure he'd hit her, but she'd walked into his fist, not that he'd aimed for her. And she had been behind in her rent, several months' worth as a matter of fact. But he had paid that off, hadn't he? When were people going to realize that he was just an innocent bystander in all of this and stop making him the heavy?

"What else is wrong with her besides the concussion?" He'd hit her hard, he knew it. Danburn had used a little of his beast to make his point with the man threatening her, but he'd not beaten her. There had been no time at all to check his swing, and when he'd hit her at the side of her head, he knew that she'd be in pain. The fact that she'd sat there and spoke to him, cursed him actually, made him think it hadn't been so bad.

But he'd looked at her when she'd fainted. He'd seen her arms and legs when she was out, and felt his beast roar out against it. He was going to find whoever had done this to her and make them pay. Then Tom spoke, bringing him from his fury.

"Malnourished. Underweight by a good twenty pounds. She's been hit before today too. I'd say a couple of days ago." Tom handed him a thick file. "She has a sprained wrist, not from today...ankle too. I'd say done about the same time as the wrist. Her ribs on her left side have some tenderness, and I think she might have two broken on the right."

"You think?" He explained to him why he didn't know for sure. That she had refused treatment due to lack of money and insurance. "I thought I made it clear that I was paying for her stay here. Her sister's too."

"She said…well, I won't tell you what she said about that, but you're not only not paying, but whatever the cost is so far, she'll pay it off, she told me." He asked him what she'd said. "Okay, but this is from her, not me. She said that the mother fucking lord of the castle can go fuck himself, that she is not going to be beholden to the man who closes down churches and throws orphans out on their ear. Where on earth do you suppose she got that from?"

"She knows what I do for a living." Tom laughed and nodded. "Do whatever you have to do to get her well. And if she gives you any more shit, let me know. I'll straighten her out. Christ, this is a nightmare."

"I don't think it's going to get any better." He asked Tom why not. "Your mom is here. And she doesn't look any happier than the woman in my emergency room."

Tom, the chicken, walked away. Danburn's mom hugged him, then asked him what was going on. But before he could tell her anything, she moved past him to the desk, so he followed.

"Hello, my dear. I was wondering which cubical Miss Barrera is in." Danburn started to tell her that she wasn't to have visitors, but his mom turned to him and he shut up. She had that look that scared even his dragon. "You will keep that tongue behind your teeth or I will snap it off like a twig, do you understand me? She's hurt, by your hand, and I will not have you adding insult to injury by you being a harpy with her. Do I make myself perfectly clear, Fletcher Danburn English?"

"Yes, ma'am. But I would like to point out that—"

Her hand coming up cut him off. Danburn had to bite his tongue hard enough to draw blood before he nodded that he'd shut up.

He went with his mom when the nurse said she'd take her back. Even before they got to the little curtained off area, Danburn could hear her. She was talking to someone, and he had a feeling it was to herself.

"Stupid moron hit me, and now I have to come up with seven hundred dollars to pay for an ambulance ride here that I don't even remember. For all I know he dragged me here by my hair and had them charge me for that instead. And I don't even have seven cents to my name, much less seven hundred dollars to pay a bill he caused me to have." He heard her moan and took a step around his mom to see what she'd done now, but she stopped him with a hand on his arm.

"Let me do this. I have no idea what it is between the two of you, but she's hurting enough without you going in there and pissing her off more. Did you really hit her?" He nodded and felt his face heat up when she tisked at him. "Danburn, what am I going to do with you?"

Before he could tell her, like he had everyone else, that it hadn't been his fault, she was moving around the curtain. He stood close to it without leaving, wanting to hear anything she said to his mother that he might need to defend himself about.

"Oh my. Oh my goodness, child." He couldn't help it. Danburn moved around the curtain and looked where his mom was looking. "Danburn, you did this? Oh, you poor baby girl. Come on child, lay down and rest."

"I'm fine, and it wasn't his fault. Not entirely." He wondered how the hell she was standing, and started toward her to insist that she sit down. "Don't you dare touch me. I don't know what it is about you, but whenever you're close to me, I want to smack the shit out of you. And I'm too hurt right now to do more than cry."

"Sit down." He watched her struggle with his command.

"Please. Will you please sit down before you fall on your ass?"

"You were nearly nice there for a second. I guess all that meanness can only let you be that way for short spurts before you revert back to your normal self." She sat down and he noticed that she had her arms full of her clothing. "I just need a minute. Then I'm out of here."

"You're not going anywhere." He glanced at his mom when she spoke. "Danburn, go and get that nice doctor friend of yours. Have him set up a lovely room for Miss Barrera, and see if he can get her something for pain, please. And Kendrick...can I call you that? I want you to get back in this bed and rest. You're as pale as those sheets there, and I won't have you falling down again. Not while I'm here. Danburn, why are you still standing there?"

Danburn wasn't fooled. This was no more a request for him to do this than when he'd requested that Kendrick sit down. When he looked at the woman in question, he wondered again how she was even up and around.

The entire side of her head was swollen. Her eye was closed, puffed out so much that it looked like she had a growth under it. Her cheek was black and blue from the hairline to her chin, and even on her neck. The lower lip looked like she'd gone a few rounds with a prize fighter, and her upper one was split in three places, with neat stitches it in. Even her left cheek was puffed out, and he could see blood in her eye too. When she slumped forward in the chair, he moved to catch her before she fell, only to see that she was out. Danburn looked at his mom.

"I can't tell you how sorry I am that I hurt her." She told him he should be telling Kendrick that, not her. "Tom, he said that she'd been hurt before. I swear to you, if that fucking shit that tried to hurt her did that, he's done."

41

"Put her in the bed, dear, and we'll watch over her." He lifted her up as gently as he could to get a better grip on her. She still moaned, and he wanted to sit in the chair with her and hold her, keeping her safe from the monsters, ones like him. "I have some information on her if you wish it. Noah gave it to me when you called him to come to the hospital."

He put Kendrick in the bed just as a nurse came in with AMA papers. He told her that Kendrick wasn't leaving against medical advice, but he thanked her. He also requested a private room, as well as any medications that she had turned down before.

"There is a pain med, but she refused that. Lord English, if I was her, I'd be wanting it all." He nodded and told her to do what she had to do. In ten minutes there was an IV in Kendrick's arm, as well as some medications dripping into the bigger bag of fluids. An hour later he was with her when they moved her to a room and set her up for a longer stay. She was going to be pissed when she woke up. He asked his mom what Noah had told her.

"Her mother died about five years ago, alone in a hospital that she'd been checked into by Louisa. Not that Kendrick's situation changed much. From what I understand she has been taking care of her older sister since she was about seventeen and Louisa got into trouble with her then boyfriend." He asked why. "The mother, Nettie Barrera, wasn't any better than Louisa is. Worse if you ask me. Trying one scheme after another. Couldn't hold down a job, nor save a penny to pay the bills. The first five years of Kendrick's life, they moved around more often than not to skip out on rent and other money that they might owe someone. They lived in cars, ate from trashcans, and did about every other thing you can think of to survive. Then Kendrick wasn't a part of their lives for about four years. Wouldn't even go to see her at the hospital when she died. And for all the years in between then and her death, very little contact was made between the two of them that Noah could find."

He looked over at the woman and asked his mom if she knew why. He'd read a story about the mother and the attempted murder just this morning, he told his mom, but it hadn't said who it was.

"It wouldn't, I guess. Not back then. I'm still having Noah look into the details. I'm sure that whatever happened, there was money and drugs involved." Danburn wasn't sure what to believe about any of them. "You're going to help her, aren't you, Danburn? She is going to need you."

"Me? Her family is in trouble and she just takes off and leaves them. What sort of person does that?" She reached into her purse and handed him a sheet of paper. He didn't even look at it. "What is that? You're going to tell me that she had her reasons? That family in this case didn't matter?"

"Yes, I am. Kendrick was shot when she was ten, when her mother's boyfriend had had enough of sharing his place with three people who weren't giving him what he thought they should. She spent seven months in the hospital, and in that time, her mother and sister packed up and left town, without so much as a visit to make sure she lived." He looked down at the paper. It was an arrest warrant for her mother. "Nettie was told, according to the police report, to shoot her daughters and she could stay with him. The only one that she was able to shoot was that woman there. Shot her in the head twice and left her for dead."

He read the entire warrant, then looked at Kendrick again. Shot in the head. Broken ribs now, sprained wrist and ankle. A concussion, as well as numerus stitches in her beaten body, and still she came to the rescue of her sister when she needed her. He felt like a fool.

"'Every so often, someone comes along that has the heart and will of a dragon. When you find them, protect them with your life. Because you never know when greatness will come for you again.'" He looked at his mom when he quoted the saying that his father had said daily to him. "Do you suppose this is the greatness he spoke of?"

"I don't know, son. I really don't. But I think that we've only scratched the surface on how her life has been up until now." He nodded and looked back at Kendrick. "You go on back to work now. I'll stay with her for a time."

He didn't want to, but knew that his mom was right. Even with a cleared day, he had things to get done. Sitting around watching someone sleep wasn't going to get them done either. So, kissing his mom on the cheek, he left. Danburn wondered what the hell he was getting into, but made arrangements to have an entire background check done on the Barrera women. Including the mother. He was going to get to the bottom of this if it was the last thing he did.

~~~

Noah read over the papers twice more before he leaned back in his chair. He'd been working for the English family since long before either this Danburn or any of the others — except the first one — had been born, and this was the first time in his life that he didn't want to give them the information that they wanted. Well, what the youngest Danburn wanted. He glanced at the picture of the little girl in the picture and shivered. She looked...dead.

It was a picture of Kendrick when she'd been found on the floor of the apartment. The neighbors had called the police when they'd heard the gunshots being fired, and then a woman and a child had fled the place. The first officer on duty had cradled young Kendrick in his arms until the ambulance had arrived, telling her to hang on, that he had her. The first medic had snapped several pictures when he got there. This one had been in her file.

The paperwork on the shooting of Kendrick had been difficult to find. And even what little he'd been able to unearth left more questions than answers. Then he remembered that Joe Bens, a man he'd known for years, worked in records at the same hospital that Kendrick had been taken to when she'd been shot all those years ago.

"Yeah, I can send you copies of the entire file if you want." He said that he did and thanked him. "I remember her. The little girl. Poor thing. They didn't think she'd live through the night, much less longer. Her momma had put the bullets in her head, then ran off instead of paying up for what she'd done to her daughter. The only reason we even knew what had happened was the boyfriend was pissy about the girl leaving a mess to clean up and her momma running off. Cold as a fish, if you ask me."

"Why did she do it? Do you know for sure?" Joe told him what he'd read in the police report he'd found just today. That she'd needed a place to sleep, and her then boyfriend had told her to kill the girls and she could stay. "And so she shot her daughter and figured that no one would care? What sort of mother does that to her own daughter?"

"She said she was supposed to kill the other one too, but thought it might be too hard on her not to have her baby girl with her. But times, she told them when Kendrick was dying and they went there to arrest her for it, were hard." Noah asked if he knew why she'd not been arrested at the time of the shooting. "She got away. When they were carting up the little girl to take her away, she just slipped out the back door and they didn't have any way of tracking her. Not like they do now. She kept off the grid, like she was one of them agents that go deep undercover."

It appeared that Joe was right. It wasn't until her body had shown up at a hospital five years ago, riddled with cancer and well beyond any help, that anyone knew that the woman living for the most part under a bridge, was wanted for attempted murder. She'd even confessed, sort of, to having shot Kendrick, but said that Kendrick shouldn't have left her out there all alone. She'd said to the police it was Kendrick's duty as her daughter to care for her, not leave her to rot like she did. Noah thought he might have done the same under the circumstances.

Now he had not just the medical records of Kendrick, but also glossy pictures of the injuries to her little body as well. Back then there were real photographs, not digital. He picked up the one of her laying on the gurney with tubes in her mouth and blood all over the pillowcase under her. It didn't even have to be in color for Noah to know that it was blood.

"What did you find that has you so upset?"

He looked at Mary when she sat down across from him. They were friends, good friends, and he knew that telling her anything would go no further than if he'd told the chair she was sitting in. But he didn't want to tell her about the girl in the hospital. Not about her life until now, nor the things she'd done to keep her sister safe. But Noah also knew that if he didn't tell her, he'd not be able to get the weight of it off his chest.

So, Noah told her everything he'd been able to find out, speculated on the things that he wasn't sure of, and even showed her the pictures that he knew would haunt him for decades to come. When he had exhausted all his knowledge to her about Kendrick, she sat there with a tear-stained face and a look of pure horror in her eyes.

"The master, he know all this yet?" Noah told her that he did not, not yet at any rate. "You must tell him. Today, before she gets it in her head to run again. Because you know as well as I do that she's gonna. A past like this, she can't be too trusting of people with the things that have happened to her, do you think?"

"Why do you think that?" She looked down at the picture she still held in her hand, and he wondered what she was thinking. "Mary, she's too hurt to run very far. Why do you think I need to do this now? Today?"

"No one has been good to her for her whole life. Mr. English, he's a good man, but stern and a little bossy. She's got herself a temper that can match his, don't you think?" He nodded, not sure where she was going with this. "You think they can get together? The two of them. Fire on fire?"

"You mean as a couple?" She nodded. "Oh, I don't think that would work. She's…well, you know as well as I do that he's royalty and not prone to taking on causes that involve anyone like her. And that would be what it was for him, a cause. He'd want to fix her up and make her better off. Not that I think she'd let him, but you can't expect him to want to be with someone like her. It's not the way he does things."

"You're saying that he's a snob." It wasn't a question, but he answered her yes anyway. "Good. Might be that she'll take exception to that too. Never seen a man so bent out of shape over a woman before, have you? I mean, he goes by the hospital to talk to her daily. Then he comes here and complains about her like he has this problem with her. I think he's sweet on her and just doesn't know it yet."

Mary got up to work on dinner. Noah wasn't sure what to think about her declaration. His lordship and a person who flipped burgers? Never would anything work between them. Yes, he did complain about her stubbornness a great deal. And it had been hard on Noah to not say that he thought them a great deal alike. But as a couple? No, that would not do. Not at all.

He gathered up his information and put it into neat piles to give to Danburn when he returned home. Noah would catch himself thinking about the two of them together and the volatile way they seemed to be when in the same room. Whatever would they do if they were to have sex?

"Not even going to think about that." He looked up when Lady English asked him what he wasn't going to think about. "Nothing important, my lady. Just mulling over something that Mary said. About his lordship."

"If it's about him and Kendrick getting together, it's something I've been thinking about all day. Can you imagine the two of them wed?" Her suggestion shocked him so badly that he nearly told her to shut up. "And their children? Oh my, Noah, we'd have our work cut out for us if they had children like them."

"My lady, she's not even in the same class as him. I mean, she can't even pay her own bills. And Danburn? He's...he's beyond wealthy." She looked at him with a cocked brow. "I'm sorry, my lady, I just never expected you to condone such a union. They're nothing at all alike when it comes to their class."

"No. And I do believe that is what would make them a wonderful couple." She crossed her arms over her chest as she looked at him. Noah had a sudden thought that Danburn was more like her than he'd ever been his father. "You, my kind sir, are a snob."

"I am. And I am proud of it. But the two of them? I don't think that would work at all, do you?" She told him that he'd said that, and she did believe they could. "Well, I believe it bears saying again. The two of them would not suit. Perhaps, as Mary said, they would come together sexually in a way that would be epic, but not as man and wife. She wouldn't even know how to act at a dinner party. I think that she would bring an embarrassment down on his head that would be talked about for centuries."

He thought he'd made his point and finished putting his work together. When he laid it all out on Danburn's desk so that he could see it first thing, he decided that enough time had been wasted on the subject. But he could not get that nagging thought out of his head. The two of them as man and wife?

"Here." He looked at his ladyship when she shoved a picture at him. He took it but didn't have a chance to look at it before she started speaking again. "He was nothing more than a man who sold hot cinders to the rich. Most often they would kick him in the head and not pay him for what he did for them. There were no matches, no electric to get a house warm. Nothing but a fireplace and a man who sold cinders as a living. He was less than that young woman is now when I met him. Yet he never once embarrassed me like you have shamed me just this moment."

"My lady, I never meant to—"

She cut him off. "You never meant to say my husband wasn't good enough for me? You didn't mean to belittle the fact that she works hard every day, sometimes not even getting to lay her head on her own pillow because she works so many jobs? You didn't mean to classify her as nothing, not even worthy of carrying a hot coal into the house that I live in?" He knew she was mad and again tried to tell her he was sorry. "Danburn should be so lucky for her to fall in love with him. I have never seen a woman, in all my life mind you, that has made me so proud and ashamed of myself at the same time. If I worked half as hard as her, I could accomplish many things."

She was leaving the room when he looked at the picture in his hands. It was one that he'd seen many times over the centuries, one that he'd painted himself. It was a hand-painted picture of the lady and her late husband, looking at each other, so much in love that one could almost feel it coming from them. Running his finger over the dried paint, he thought of how the master of the house would have reacted to such news as his only son marrying a commoner. *He would have thought it was the best thing in the world*, Noah thought. He could almost hear him now.

"Why, can you think of the stock they would bring to the table? Strong bloodlines are hard to come by." He thought of the words that the then master of the family used to say. Noah thought it a perfect description of the young woman. *Every so often, someone comes along that has the heart and will of a dragon. When you find them, protect them with your life. Because you never know when greatness will come for you again.* He wondered if she was that greatness.

At a little past eight Danburn came home. He was in a foul mood, so Noah stayed in the kitchen with Mary. When he thought he heard him at the stairs, he made his way to the office to see if he'd left him any work. But he was sitting at his desk with the file in his hand, staring out the window. He didn't even turn when Noah said his name.

"I find myself wanting to be with her. Even with her temper driving me insane, I want to aggravate her into a frenzy just to see her cheeks get all pink and her eyes burn with it." Noah said nothing, but did look at the picture that was still sitting on the corner of his desk. "Tonight she told me to get out and to never return. I stayed just to see if she'd let me kiss her. Kiss her. Like she wouldn't try and tear my throat out if I got too close."

"Perhaps you should try charming her." Danburn turned and looked at him. "She has not had many people try to be nice to her. It might put her off, but then again, she might enjoy a little pampering from the right man."

"I've been thinking of my father a lot today. And her. He would have loved her, you know that, don't you? Mother already does." Noah nodded and sat in the chair. "They're releasing her tomorrow and I'm going to bring her here. Her sister is going to be a bit longer, but Kendrick is coming here so I can keep an eye on her."

"She won't like that." Danburn nodded. "Where shall I put her? On the upper floors or on the family floor close to you?"

Danburn said nothing for several minutes. Noah had a feeling that he was trying to figure out if he wanted her that close to him or not. Noah, like the rest of the household, was beginning to think that they might be good for each other. He wasn't sold on marriage, but he could see how they'd be good together on other levels.

"Put her in the room across from mine. That way if she tries to run, I can hear her." Noah nodded. "And she'll need things too. I haven't any idea what that might entail, but could you get with my mom and see if she'll give you a list of items a woman might need to have while recuperating?"

"Yes, sir." Noah wanted to ask him if he was ready for this, to have a stranger living here full time, but he didn't. He was pretty sure that Danburn wouldn't have an answer any more than he did. "What of Ms. James?"

"We're to take care of her in the morning. Everything is set up for it to happen." Danburn leaned back and looked older all of a sudden. "Do you think I'm going to live to regret this, Noah?"

"No. I have no idea why, but I'm beginning to think this might be the best thing for all of us." Danburn nodded and smiled at him. "What shall I tell the staff regarding her? I mean, there will be questions."

"I'm sure there will be. I have a few of my own. But I have no idea. She's…nothing to me at the moment. Can we just leave it at that?" Noah nodded and thought about the closing of the house in a few days.

"Sir, the household. We're to leave in three days. Do we stay or…? There is also the matter of your apartment and the things that were to be taken from here to there. I don't think there is a second room there for the young miss."

"No, there's not. And for now…for now we're going to put off the closing of the house." Noah nodded, feeling relieved about the decision. "Find someone to help Kendrick. I don't mean a maid or whatever they're called now, but someone just to help her out."

Noah wasn't sure that was going to work out well either, but said he'd do it. As he was leaving the office, thinking of all the things he had to do tomorrow, he made his way to the kitchen to talk to Mary. She was going to gloat. There was no help for it, but in this he was pretty sure that she had hit the nail on the head.

# Chapter 4

Kendrick wasn't sure she wanted to be here, but as the doctor explained, there was no help for it. The shelter was out of the question, not just because he said so but because she wasn't going to go there again. And she needed a place to recuperate. The master of the house had asked, not ordered, her to come here. Looking around the room, she wondered what the hell kind of money it took to buy and keep a castle running. The knock at the door had her covering her legs up and telling the person to enter.

"Miss. You may remember that my name is Noah, and I work for Mr. English, Danburn. I'll be helping you with a few things for today to get you settled. Starting tomorrow I have hired a nurse to come in and care for you, but after that, we'll have to figure out who can take over my duties for you." She nodded, not sure what he was talking about. "There is also the matter of the milliner. She would like to come in on Thursday to see about—"

"The milliner?" He told her what it meant. "I know what a milliner is, Noah. What I meant was, why do I need a person to come in and make me clothing? I have some that are perfectly fine at my...I had some at the apartment. I have no idea what happened to them. But as I'm not going to be here that long, I don't need someone to make me anything."

"I'm afraid that the local store will not carry the sort of dress you will need should there be a gathering." She had to ask him what that meant too. "A dinner party. Danburn has them on occasion, and you might be required to host one for him."

"Host a party for him. I see. Well, not really, but I'm beginning to get an idea. You think I'm going to be here for the master. His plaything, as it were." She almost felt sorry for Noah but moved on, wanting to clear the air before things got out of hand. "I've no intentions of fucking the master of the house, no matter how much he pays for me to stay here. I will be perfectly fine living in my car. I have no idea where it is right now, but I could easily have lived there for a long time without having to put out for a man like him."

"I'm not...I didn't mean to imply that you would. It was my understanding that...." He looked so helpless that she thought the man was going to blow a gasket. "Miss, I swear to you, I never meant for you to think you had to pay for staying here by sleeping with the master."

"Good. So long as we're on the same page on that." He nodded and sat down on the pretty blue wingback by the fireplace. "Why am I in this room? I mean, there has to be a smaller, less done up room than this one that I could be staying in. I'm not a guest, and I certainly don't need all this room."

"I was told to put you here." Kendrick asked him by who. "The master of the house. He wanted you close in the event that you tried to run."

She knew that he'd said too much the moment he slapped his hand over his mouth. But she wanted answers, and if she had to make him tell her the truth, then she was all right with that too. Kendrick was pissed off. More than that, she wanted to hunt down Danburn right now and demand that he put her in one of the less…well, pretty rooms. She was going to get to the bottom of this right now.

"Where is he?" Noah said he was in his office. "Is that somewhere here in this house, or has he gone to his office in the city?"

"Here, my lady. He is here. He is taking an at home day today to make sure that you have settled in well." He looked poleaxed. "I find that I cannot lie to you."

"Yes, I know." As she tossed back the covers again, she reached for the oversized shirt she'd managed to get someone to bring her from her home when she'd been in the hospital. Kendrick wasn't sure what had happened to the rest of her things. There really wasn't that much, but she knew that someone had picked it up and taken it out of the apartment. Going to the door, she nearly fell back when it was jerked open and the man himself was standing there.

"You are not going to be my lover, and I will not be fucking you so long as I can move away from you. Do you hear me?" He looked at her with a shocked look, and she felt her face heat up. "What I meant to say was, I'm not going to be letting you sleep with me so that I can have a nice place to sleep. In fact, I want you to find me a smaller room, one that is more suitable for someone like me."

"And what sort of person are you? I mean, I want to get this right the first time with you. I have a feeling that you won't let me live it down if I don't." She watched as Noah slipped out of the room, closing the door behind him. Coward. "Did you have perhaps a hovel in mind? I assure you that I have no rooms on the estate like that."

"Don't you have a maid's room or something I can use until I'm ready to get set free?" He took a step closer to her and she backed away. "Maybe I can stay in like, a pool house or something."

"The pool house is currently occupied by the pool equipment. And I don't have a maid, I have a butler." Two more steps back to his two toward her. "I do have another room in mind, but I don't think you're going to like it any better than you do this one."

"Your room." He nodded, and she felt the bed railing touch the back of her legs. "You're not going to sleep with me."

"No, I'm not." She felt the air swoosh out of her. "When we come together, there will be very little sleep for either of us, I think. Or at least I hope so."

"You can't want to sleep with me." He shook his head, but the smile on his face made her think he was still on the little sleep comment. "I'm not having sex with you. I don't like you."

"Yes, you've told me. I, however, find you to be very appealing. I have thought of little else but the need to see if your body is as pretty as I think it is." Kendrick looked for a way to escape, but he cut even that off by putting his hands on either side of her, using the footboard. "You have a very sexy mouth. I bet it tastes good too."

"You can't be serious." He was apparently, and lowered his head to hers. "I'm not going to allow you to kiss me. I don't like you."

"So you keep saying." But the moment his mouth brushed

over hers, it was all Kendrick could do not to grab his arms and pull him closer. "Let me kiss you, Kendrick. Let me taste the darkness of your mouth."

The matter was taken out of her hand when he curled his hand at the back of her head and slowly pulled her to him. Licking her lips, wanting to feel his lips upon hers, she watched him as he moved to her. Even his eyes, a dark purple in color, seemed to say something to her.

"This is a terrible idea." If he answered, she had no clue, because then his mouth was taking hers. And take it he did.

She knew he was being careful of her lips. They were still sore, but not nearly as swollen. Her eye, too, was much better and she could see out of it, but it, too, was painful sometimes. But he ran his hand down her back, touching her spine all the way to her ass, and she moaned loudly against his mouth when he cupped her and pulled her to him. Every thought she'd ever had of turning this man down flew right out the window.

Her feet no longer touched the floor. Her breasts were pressed hard against his chest, and she knew that he could feel her nipples as they hardened. She could feel his too, and moved her hand to the one at her left and pinched it gently in her fingers. He jerked his mouth from hers and looked down at her.

"Do you have any idea what you're doing to me?" She nodded, then shook her head. "Yes, that about covers it for me too."

When he put her down and took a step back from her, removing not only his hands from her but his heat as well, Kendrick felt cold, bereft, and out of sorts. When he took another step or two back, she held onto the footboard again and tried to sum up some anger. But there wasn't any anger.

Confusion yes, a little hurt too. But no anger.

"Don't do that again." He shook his head at her. "I mean it. Don't you dare kiss me again. I told you, I'm not going to be your sexual plaything while I'm here. It's not what I want from you."

"I don't want that either. You as my sexual plaything, I mean. But if I took you in my arms right now, would you let me lay you out on that bed and eat you?" Her body heated up; her pussy gushed. "I can smell you, Kendrick. You might say one thing, but your body says something entirely different."

"I know my head, and it is saying for you to keep your distance. I don't want you any more than you want me. I'm just here. And that's all there is to it." Danburn closed the distance between them in two steps. Her body was wrapped around his, her ankles locked at his hips. He pressed her against the wall, having moved across the room to do so. She cried out when he rocked into her heated flesh, her pussy on fire for him.

"Come for me. Come now." She tried to think of anything but doing what he wanted. But the harder he rocked into her, the more she needed to let go. The entire time he watched her, his eyes locked on hers. "Come, Kendrick. Come apart now."

Her body did just that. It seemed to not just come apart for him, but did so several times in a row until she was weak with it. But he wasn't finished with her. As he continued to rock into her, bringing her body close to the edge again, he told her all the things he was going to do to her, and how much she was going to enjoy them. When he was finished with her, and there wasn't any doubt to her that it was his decision, not hers, he stopped moving against her and took a step back.

"That was a mistake. I shouldn't have allowed it to go that far." She felt her heart tear; her blood simply stopped flowing to the wound in her chest that had once been her beating heart. "We barely know each other, and here we are having sex like animals against the wall, for Christ's sake."

This time when he set her on the floor, she staggered slightly and he reached for her. Kendrick slapped his hands away from her. And when he tried again, she slapped him on the face. Her anger burned through her like her blood had only moments ago when she'd come for him.

"Did you enjoy that? Do you feel like the powerful king of the castle now that you've made the poor girl feel like a woman?" He opened his mouth and she snapped at him. "Yes, so I came, thank you for that. How lovely of you to make me feel like a whore in your home. Will there be any other services that I can provide for you, Master English? Perhaps I can drop down and suck you off while you lord your superiority over me."

"I wasn't...I didn't mean for that to happen." Kendrick made her way back to the bed, her heart broken into pieces. "I'm sorry. I only meant to kiss you and leave."

"You had your kiss. Now if you don't mind, I'd like to be alone."

He didn't say anything, and she didn't look in his direction. Her mind was on a loop right now, and his words, that it had been a mistake, didn't make her feel any better about what had happened and how she felt right now.

~~~

Danburn stood outside her room for twenty minutes, trying to figure out what he could do now. He'd hurt her. He knew that as surely as he was standing there. But how to fix it was something that was beyond him. Then as he stood there, thinking that he should go in and talk to her, he heard the sobs from the other side of the door and he leaned against it. Now he'd made her cry. His mother's voice from down the hall had him going to her like she was a lifeline.

"I made her cry. How do I stop it? I only wanted a little kiss. Well, that's not true. I wanted her. I guess that's too much to tell my mother, but I made her cry and I don't know what to do about it. Help me." She looked at him like...well, like she didn't have any idea who he was. "Kendrick. I made her cry by kissing her. Well, not the kissing part. I think she enjoyed that, but now she's crying and I don't know how to fix it."

"What did you say to her?" He told her everything, even the part where he'd nearly taken her against the wall. "So you manhandled her, then told her that you'd messed up and called her an animal."

"It sounds much worse when you say it like that." His mom just stared at him. "Okay, it is much worse now that I say it aloud. I only meant that.... Christ, I have no idea what I meant. Only that I wanted her later and not while she was hurting like she is."

"That would have been a better way to tell her than you think she's an animal." He didn't think he'd called her that, but his mother was helping right now and he didn't want her upset too. "Do you have any idea how to grovel? Or to be romantic? I've never seen you do it, but I think you might have picked up a thing or two from your dad. Maybe."

"I can grovel. You make me.... I mean, I do it when I need to, when I've messed up with you. And I am romantic. Women love me." She looked at him, cockeyed. "Mother, I'm a drowning man here. I want her to not cry. It makes me feel… like I've gotten hurt myself."

"Yes, I'm sure it does." Danburn wasn't sure what she meant, but before he could ask, she continued. "Grovel. Buy her flowers. No, not flowers, but plants. I think she'd be the one person in the world who would want a rose bush rather than a dozen roses. But then she'd not know where to plant them. I'll have to think on that. But you can be kind to her. No more ordering her about like she's the animal you called her."

"I didn't call her an animal." His mother cocked her impressive brow at him. "Well, I didn't. I said simply that I wasn't going to take her like one. There is a marked difference in that."

"Not to her." Okay, he could see her point in that. But he still had no idea how to make her not hate him. And for a reason that he couldn't, or maybe didn't want to, explain to himself, he didn't want her to hate him. "Go to work for now. I'll make sure that she's cared for today. You must, however, think of every little thing you can do to make this work with her, Danburn. I like this girl a great deal, and I don't want you to mess it up."

As soon as he got to work he sat at his desk and began looking up things about being a romantic. He found a great deal of speculation on how that could work for men. Danburn wasn't sure any of it would work on Kendrick, but he made notes. At several points while he was working quietly at his desk, he considered calling her and asking her what she wanted. But he knew that most of the time, women had no idea what they wanted. He'd read that several times now as he worked through the information on the computer.

When Noah came in a little before noon to go with him to two meetings, one of which was going to involve Julia and her brother, he asked him what Kendrick was doing. He didn't seem to want to answer him, kept fobbing him off on other information that he didn't need. Finally, he told him to tell him.

"She's very delicate." Not a word he might have used for

her, but he listened to his friend. "I don't mean in the fragile sort of way, even though there are times when she is that as well. But what I mean is she's not had anything nice done for her or given to her. I would imagine all her life. And when she sees something, like the cut flowers in the hall that were put out this morning, she went on and on at their fragrance and color. The beautiful way that Beth had put the colors together to make them seem brighter. I sent her to the yard with Pierce to have him show her the castle walls. I know I find them beautiful."

"I like her." Noah said that he'd figured that out. "No. I mean I really like her. She's not like the other women I've met. She's straightforward and doesn't seem to care that I'm a lord with money. Of course it's never come up, but I have a feeling that should it, she'd just tell me to fuck off."

"She would at that. I think, and I have less experience with women than you, but I do think she's like a breath of fresh air." Noah looked slightly embarrassed for a moment, but continued. "I had it in my head that she wasn't good enough for you. Not in any way but as a bed partner. But I have since changed my mind into thinking—and please do not take this the wrong way—but I'm thinking that you're not good enough for her."

It hurt. He would only admit that to himself, but he thought Noah was right. He'd been overbearing to her. Mean even. Ordering her about like she was a minion. And the incident in the bedroom had shown him that he wanted more from her than just a good fuck. He wanted to make love to her.

The meeting seemed to go on for hours with Conrad, Julia's brother, and his lawyer. They thought that since he had the money that they should be able to go on as usual. He, however, thought that he should keep his money and bring in some of his own people to run the place. After he spent a fortune in getting things up to code. The complex of new homes was nearly in ruins when he'd stepped in.

Four weeks ago he'd bought the bank note on two housing developments. One was in the upper side of town, the other mid-range income homes. Most of the houses were empty, the work done on them shoddy and short. As he walked through the house they were using as a demo, he started snapping pictures to compare to the ones he knew were to be sold to the public. The man with them and his attorney had taken exception to that.

"There is no reason to think that the other homes are going to be this nice. That's just not the way that things are done around here." He asked them why not. "Well, this is a model of what they can be doing to them, not what we have done in them. Of course this house is going to look better. People who buy them should figure that out right away."

"No, this house should be the same as the one that they're buying. When you put this model home here, to let them see what you're selling, it should be the same if not less than what the consumer gets." He pulled up a picture that he'd taken a couple of weeks ago when the paperwork had been approved for his purchase. "This is the house that is currently on the market. What do you think the person who has paid for the model home does when he gets in his home and finds that he not only has no countertops in his kitchen and baths, but that the flooring is only subflooring and that the walls aren't painted? I would be very upset with you and demand my money returned to me. I do believe that's why you're behind in your payments here, as well as having several clients suing you."

"Well, then you should fix them. That's what you bought

the notes for, isn't it? To own all this and have an income from the houses. But I have a better idea than that. One that I think you're going to do." Danburn said nothing but looked at Noah. "You have all the money now. And my bank loans. I can't sell the houses, as you said, the way they are. So fix them up, and then we'll be able to sell them for you while taking a cut."

"*We'll* be able to sell them? I don't think so. No, what is going to happen is, you're going to leave the premises, and I'm going to bring in a crew to settle these homes up and then sell them on my own. I told you when you made this appointment to talk to me that your services were no longer required." The man only huffed at him. "Perhaps I didn't make myself clear on this."

"Oh, you were very clear. But we're not leaving. What you paid off, that doesn't give us back what we invested of our own money in this venture. We're staying. As I told you before you purchased this out from under us, we are part of the deal." Danburn nodded to Noah, who slipped out of the room as the man continued. "You either play ball our way so that we can make money, or we come in, destroy everything here, and you're left with shit to sell."

Conrad smiled at him. Danburn felt his beast run along his skin to let him know he was there if he needed him. When Noah returned and nodded back at him, Danburn stretched his neck and heard it pop twice before he looked at the man and his lawyer, who hadn't said a word since this thing started.

"You can do this my way or you can be arrested, Conrad. You have less than five minutes to get into your expensive car and get out, or I will, as I have told you I would do, have you arrested for trespassing." Conrad only nodded, smiling at him like he had a great secret. "You won't have to worry about the office equipment being gathered, by the way. The Feds have been going through that since we arrived, and left there."

"What do you mean, the Feds?" The lawyer finally seemed to wake up and looked panicky as he turned to his client. "You didn't tell me that there would be Federal officers involved. You said this would be a simple case of bullying a rich man into getting your money back. I told you when you called me yesterday that this wouldn't work. I've known Danburn for years, and he does not walk away from a deal. As of right now, Conrad, I'm finished. I'll send you a bill for my services, but this is the stupidest thing you've ever done as far as I'm concerned."

The attorney—and Danburn could not for the life of him remember his name—waved at his ex-client as he left them standing there. When Conrad turned back to him, Danburn had a feeling that the man was going to try something very stupid, and watched him as he smiled.

"You can't do shit to me. And you're going to do just what I tell you to do and keep your mouth shut about it. Would you like to know why?" Danburn nodded. "Because I have something that you want. And you want it badly. You might say I have an ace up my sleeve when it comes to having dealings with men like you."

"And what would that be?" Danburn had a few things that he wanted. One of them was currently in his home, injured and upset with him. But there was nothing that this man could do for him or get for him that Danburn had on his list. "You have no money and the car you drove here has been repossessed as of now. Your home, used as collateral on the development you have across town, is now in the hands of the bank. The few friends that you had have long since told you to fuck off, and you couldn't borrow the money for a newspaper if they were giving them away. Whatever do you think you might have that I'd want?"

"Why, I have Julia James. You remember her, don't you? The woman that you have been dating for a few years now? I have her, and if you ever want to see her again, you'll sign the paperwork I have here now." Danburn said nothing as Conrad produced several sheets of folded paper from his pocket. "Just sign where the markers are and this will end nicely for all of us. Julia is currently hidden away and ready to be given back to you once you do as you're told and put me and my company in charge."

"Really? Then let me talk to her." He was shaking his head even before Danburn finished speaking. "So, on blind trust that you have her, I'm supposed to just sign off on this paperwork and let you ruin me. Because as much as I don't trust you now, I doubt that things will get any better between us. How much more are you going to try and get from me, Conrad? Millions? More? Tell me."

"You never know what I might want in the future from you. I might just let you off with only making you pay me an upfront amount of five million, or I might want five mill a month for the next fifty years. By the way, that's in the paperwork too, that I can get money from you whenever I see fit." Danburn said nothing as the man stood there. "Well?"

"Well what?" He asked him if he was going to sign the paperwork to get Julia back. "No. I don't work that way, and if you thought I did, then you're stupider than we all thought. And let me tell you, I knew how stupid you were from the beginning. Who builds a housing development like this? There are no roads here. No kind of entertainment for the masses. Or did you expect them to spend all their time fixing up the pieces of shit that you sold them? That's it, isn't it?"

"I don't really care what they do with their time so long as they don't come to me whining about what I did or didn't do. That'll be your problem from now on. But back to Julia. You'd just let her die? Because you think you're better than me? I think not." Danburn didn't answer him. There was no way that he'd kill her, he knew that for a fact. Nor did he have her hidden away. "I can't believe the great Danburn English would just let a woman die over money."

"You are. Not me." He stood there for several more minutes, and could tell that Conrad was nervous. For the first time that day, Danburn felt within his element. Wanted to shout to the world that things were going his way for a change. As he rocked on his heels, waiting for the man to take some sort of action, he kept an eye on Noah as well.

Noah was an immortal, much like he was. They could die, yes, his father had proven that for them, but it was harder to do so and they lived forever. Noah, because of his relationship with Danburn, would of course live forever too. But he did have limitations that Danburn didn't. And they were great.

Noah couldn't change into a dragon, for one thing. There wasn't any magic that he could use, as Danburn and his kind could. And for most shifters he knew, with age came the added abilities afforded to them. More magic being one of them. So he kept an eye on his friend in the event that Conrad got any dumber. He didn't want anyone to get hurt if he could help it.

Danburn, with just a wave of his hand, could kill a waterway or give it as much life as it could hold. His scales, in his dragon form, could heal lakes and oceans, as well as the earth surrounding it. His castle, the one that he'd built when he'd come of age, was the result of some of that magic. It was the main reason it butted up against the large mountain. He was, when you thought about it, a part of the waterways that ran beneath the mountain as much as he was the stone and grounds around it. It was safe there, not just for him and his mother, but those that lived and worked there. Danburn took care of his own.

The Feds moved just past the doorway as Conrad started naming off all the things that he was going to take from him. Danburn knew that Noah had called them in, and now that they were here, he could do just what he'd been asked to do. Get the man to confess to his crimes. It was sort of a letdown, he supposed. He had wanted to hurt the man for what he and his sister had done. Noah gave him the thumbs up, and he looked at the man in front of him.

"Julia is in custody." Conrad started shaking his head, his body hard with fear now. "Conrad, you were never going to get away with this. You and Julia should have known better than to play a hand you had no chance of winning. And there was no way you were going to win this, no matter who you kidnapped."

"You think not? Well, that is where you're wrong. We know things about you that will ruin you when it comes out." Danburn asked him again what he thought he had. "You're a dragon. A man that can shift into a beast, and the world will know about it if you don't sign the paperwork now."

Danburn didn't even bother looking around to see who might have heard him. Instead, he threw back his head and laughed. He had no idea how they had found out, but there was no point in denying it. Nor was he going to agree with him. Conrad asked him if he'd heard him.

"Yes. A dragon, you say? Well, I suppose that's about as truthful as it comes. Tell me, Conrad, what sort of dragon am I? Do I burn villages with my hot breath? Am I the kind of dragon that sheds tears for the money that I need to take over failing business like yours? Or am I the kind of dragon that flies below the surface of the waters and eats all manner of men and women who dare venture into my territory?" All true to a point, but some of them had happened very long ago, when the world was a much different place. "I know. I'm a great silver dragon that does all those things and more. I fly the skies on cloudy days so that I can have the freedom of spreading my wings when I'm alone. I command mountains to build a castle that is as much a part of the stones that it was shaped from as the fish are to the water that holds them in its belly."

He took the necessary steps to Conrad to close the distance between them. Then he grabbed his head and pulled it to his, their foreheads touching. When he locked his eyes to his, Danburn let Conrad see him—all of him—in his glory, and what he looked like when he was pissed off. Then he let him go. Few had ever seen what he'd shown the human male. And no one would believe a word he said when he told them.

The man was still screaming when the Feds took him away. Noah stood beside him as Danburn answered all the questions the Feds had for him. Yes, he had spoken to the man about dragons. No, he had no idea where he might have gotten the information. Yes, he had agreed with him to humor him. The slightly unstable, Danburn pointed out, were prone to violence, and he was doing his best to avoid that.

After they were done, the Feds were taking the man away with his arms tied behind him, he and Noah pulled out their phones and began making the necessary calls. First and foremost, they had to get these houses up to standards, as well as getting the workers, the ones hired by Conrad, his sister, and his firm, off the property.

After that, he decided he'd had enough excitement for

one day and headed home. But he made several stops before getting there. He had a woman to woo and make happy. He thought flowers and chocolate were a good beginning.

# Chapter 5

Kendrick walked around the big stone castle and marveled at the sheer size of it. Some of the walls seemed to blend right into the mountain they were near, and she wondered if any hidden openings existed that would lead her to the middle of the mountain, or to the sublevels of the house itself. She put her hand on the wall, feeling its coolness, just as someone cleared their throat behind her. Turning, she looked at Danburn and then back at the wall.

"Are you enjoying your walk?" She moved to the other side of the garden that seemed as much a part of the castle as did the mountain itself. "Pierce said that he'd been called away and asked if I'd come out and answer your questions. He's going to be a while. One of the workers cut his hand and requires stitches."

"It's so cold here. The stone is as cold as ice." She hadn't meant to speak to him, but now that she had, she decided that he might have more information than the doctor had. "The mountain, Pierce said, rose from the ground to create the castle for you. What did he mean by that?"

"Just that. When I decided to have a home built here, the land and all the surrounding area around it was flat. It had also been over-farmed. There had been, at one time, sheep running here, but they too were dying, due to the lack of vegetation. So I made a bargain with the grounds." She stared at him. It was a fanciful story, but completely untrue. She asked him what the bargain had been. "That I would forever leave a part of me behind when I swam in the waterways, keep the hearths burning, and make sure there were people, which the land needs to survive, living peacefully with her. She was ready to agree by then, and we have lived well together since. Living in harmony here between the mountain and the lake."

"I see." Kendrick ran her hand over the beautiful pinkish stone that was a part of this side of the castle. "This is a different stone than on the other side. I guess one can't expect the earth to match everything up."

"On the contrary, she did. The reason that the stone here is a darker hue than the other side is because the dirt well below this was clay. It blended well within the stone here, and gave some of the earth below the opportunity to feel the sun on it again. Long before I built this castle, as I said, it was a dying earth." He moved up beside her, and she could feel the heat of his body with hers. "You don't believe me, do you?"

"I don't know what to believe about you." She moved away, one of the hardest things she'd ever done. "I talked to the doctor about my sister today. He said that she's doing well and should be ready to leave the hospital in a few days."

"She'll not come here, however. I think he told you that." Kendrick nodded. She really didn't want her sister here either, but there wasn't any point in explaining that to him. "She has men trying to murder her, and I would rather her be someplace that is safe for all of us. No one will find her where we put her, and she will continue to have good care as long as she does what she's told."

"She won't. But then I'm sure you already figured that out. Noah told me that he'd had me investigated. As well as Louisa." Danburn nodded but said nothing as he leaned against the stone. "I have this thing I can do. You won't have known about it when you did your research. And the only reason I'm telling you now is I don't want you to think I've harmed Noah."

"He told me that he cannot lie to you. It bothers him a great deal. Not that he would want to lie to you, but he is pressured somewhat to tell you the truth no matter how much it pains him." Kendrick leaned down to smell a small blossom. "You never pick the things here, do you? You only make note of them, then move on. Why is that?"

"If I were to pick it or even to damage it, the next person to come by wouldn't be able to enjoy what I have. It's a give and take thing for me. They give me pleasure and I give them the option of continuing. I mean, they could still die from any number of things, but this way, I've left it, in my opinion, better than most would have." He told her that was lovely of her. "No, it's just that I don't have a lot of pleasures in my life. Smelling a flower or two and leaving it behind so that I might come back to see it again is all I have."

"Tell me of this thing you can do so that he can't lie to you. Please?" She would have told him anyway, but the "please" helped her feel better about it. "You said that it was a thing you can do. Have you always been able to do that?"

"No. Just since…my mother, she tried to kill me when I was younger. The bullets were removed, of course, but while they were there, in my head, they touched off some things that hadn't been there before. Like the ability to have people not lie to me, for one." He asked her what else there was. "I can see things. With a touch I can see what its journey has been since its creation. Not people, just things. Loose change, a blanket left behind. Sometimes I can see the owner of an object, but not much more than that."

"And the stone you touched, could you see its journey too?" She told him that the stone did not want her to see. "I don't understand you. You mean things can block you?"

"Sort of. The stone is large, bigger than I am. Its collective thoughts, I guess you can call it, are stronger than me. I think I could force my way in, see what I want, but I won't. If it's not mine for the taking, then I move on." She looked at Danburn and wondered when he'd moved so close to her. "I think she doesn't want me to see for fear of how I will react."

"And if she gives you permission now, would you look?" His voice, not like the man, was soft, gentle, and she wanted to wrap herself in it. But he'd hurt her once today, and she didn't want to feel that helpless and pain filled again. "Touch the wall now, Kendrick, and let it show you that I did not lie to you about how it came to be."

"I'm not sure I want to know." He nodded but took her hand in his. Following him to the wall, she laid her hand on the cool stone when he put it there, and closed her eyes. The warmth started first. Then the movement of time going backward made her slightly dizzy, and she nearly pulled away when it stopped.

"When I came here, as I said, the ground was dying. Can you see it?" She could, and answered Danburn's whispered question. "I have power, magic if you will, that can move mountains. I can create winds and water where none was before. I can also talk to the earth when she lets me. I am a dragon of the earth. My forefathers, all of them, once walked this land and lived with the humans. But no more. We hide in our skins so we may live and help the land that we once called home."

The earth seemed to appear before her. It was as he had said, dead. The grasses were brown, the trees, what few there were of them, were only sticks in the ground, long since having given up their leaves, their roots as dead as they were. Some small sheep were roaming, but Kendrick had a feeling that they had not seen a human for years, and that their only reason for survival was that the earth had needed them as much as they did her. Then a man, the same man standing close enough to her that she could hear his heart beating, sat down on the dead grounds and dug his hands into the earth. The ground seemed to grow around him until only his head was showing.

They sat that way, the earth and the man, until suddenly the ground below him began to quake. Grasses moved and began to turn green, roots digging deeper into the earth as she watched them. The trees, too, shifted in the dirt that held him until they were nearer to him. Then great stones began to rise up from the ground…larger than the man, larger than any building that she'd ever seen.

"The stones were there, hidden deep, the foundation that she had her life begin on. As it shifted and became something that I needed, the ground beneath turned and became fresh. Roots that had long been dormant rose up now and faced the sun with renewed life. As the land began to take on life, so did the mountain that rose up for me." The stone shifted, the one she touched now began to form rooms within its belly. Windows opened, stairs began to build from every floor above it to the ground below. Smaller stones began to move, and window seats appeared. Pools in several rooms were heated with the mountain's water, pure and clean. "The water is forever warmed to the perfect temperature. Clean, as it runs through the mountain, purifying it as it enters each room. See the fireplace? Its hearth and walls are made of the strongest rock, and they will hold heat and warmth long after the fire burns down and only cinders remain. No man can enter here or any of the rooms without permission. Either from me or the wall itself."

She felt his breath on her neck, his lips moving over her cheek as he pressed his face to hers. Kendrick wanted to turn to him, feel his mouth over hers, his body pressed against hers again. But she was also afraid of him. Not the man, but his words that could cut her again, and this time she knew that she would bleed from a wound that would not heal.

The mountain paused in its movement, seeming to take a breath as the grounds around it shifted again. A large hole opened, its depth so deep that she was sure that the castle and mountain could have hidden inside of it. Stairs led up from it at one point, reaching to the castle below the earth and connecting somehow, she knew, to the levels below the now completely formed and filling lake.

As she watched, water began to cascade into it, from all sides and even the floor. The stone of it, the bottom of the now filling lake, was as smooth as the stone of the castle, and no less beautiful. When the waters had filled in, the plant life surrounding it began to grow, taking on a life that had never been there before.

"Look at me, Kendrick. The man there, look at me and see what I truly am."

She didn't want to. She knew that once she saw him,

really saw him for what he was, she'd never be able to leave here. Not him or the castle. When he told her again, begged her to turn and look at him, she felt her body move, the earth beneath her rejoicing in what she was about to see.

~~~

Danburn held her body to his. Sheltered her, as the mountain did him, in the event it proved too much for her. The castle, the mountain, and the water all told him to do this for her, to give her a gift that no one had ever wanted or needed before. As her body turned in their combined dreams, Danburn felt his beast roar out.

He knew what he looked like when she turned. His great dragon had emerged when the earth began to move for him. He stood there, proudly now, showing this woman that he was a dragon of worth. A monster only in the hearts and fears of those who would harm her.

His mane was full of thorns, down his back from the top of his head to the tip of his tail. Wings spread now, wide and beautiful, their story there for anyone to see should they want. His scales, a silver color under battle mode, now shone brightly with the magic around him, taking on the colors and hues of every life they touched. It had served him well over the years, but now only shone for the woman who was touching his mind.

The art of his life covered every inch of his wings, as well as his heart was. Each battle was represented there, each time he'd taken a life. Some of them yet moved, the memory of them still fresh to him, showing the battle that he'd fought in, and the deaths of those that had fought beside him. Then when he lowered his body to the ground, the belly of his dragon heated up to do what was needed. He looked at Kendrick to see her face when the fire left his throat to still the stone where it lay, the heat of it making the ground where he lay with her warm so she would always be warm.

Before he could guess her intentions, she pulled from the wall and put her hands on his chest. He knew she felt his heart. The one beating hard because she'd touched him. When she licked her lips, running her tongue over their fullness, Danburn leaned in to kiss her.

The kiss was gentle, their bodies seeming to melt into one. As he brought her closer to him, his hands holding her tightly to him, Danburn felt something that he'd never felt before…a connection to another person on a level that he'd only felt with the earth. Lifting her up in his arms, he turned her to the castle again and felt her wrap around him.

"I cannot wait," he told her when he pulled his mouth free. "I need to bury myself within you."

Nodding, she began to tear at his clothing. His tie was jerked from the buttons on his shirt, his jacket was pulled down over his arms and dropped where it lay. Her own clothing suffered as much. Danburn ripped open the blouse she had on. Kendrick lifted up the bra that seemed sexy from the moment he saw it, and he pulled her breast into his mouth. Tugging at her pants, he nearly cried out when they caught. Finally he simply tore them from her, no longer caring about their fabric.

"Hurry." He grinned at her urgency. He too felt it, the need to mate, to become one. When his pants gave him fits, he pulled a little of his beast and the pants fell away in shreds. His feet were now bare of shoes and socks as he held her naked body close to his.

"I want to see you." Her head shook and he pulled her legs from behind him. "I must see you in all your glory. We, my dragon and I, we need it."

"I'm not that special." But he had her standing before him now, her body beautifully bare. "You're so big."

He looked down his own body and saw himself as she might. His cock was thick and hard, straining from his body with pre-cum at the tip. His chest was wide, devoid of hair, and his nipples, like hers, were hard. Danburn wanted to taste every part of her, drink from her nectar, and hear her scream out his name. But he needed to be inside of her more than he needed to satisfy his need of a drink.

"I should like to take you here, against the castle. Feel it behind you as I fill you." She nodded and he put out his finger to trace her collarbone to her nipple. "The thought of fucking you has my beast snarling at me to begin, but I want to give you pleasure first."

"If you do this right, I'm going to have a great deal of pleasure, I think." Her hand slipped over her mouth when she spoke, and he pulled it away. "I don't know why I said that."

"Yes you do. You are as needy as I am." Danburn ran his finger down her belly to her navel, and then played there for a moment. Her moans had him watching her face, and he almost missed what her fingers were doing.

They were at her pussy, just above her nether lips, but so very close that he wanted to beg her to dip them inside. Sliding his own fingers to match hers, he felt the heat of her pull at him when he gently parted her lips for her own fingers.

"I wish now to taste you." He dropped to his knees and licked her fingers clean after pulling them free of her soft lips. Sucking her clit into his mouth then biting down gently, he was rewarded with a mouthful of her cream and the first taste of paradise. Lifting her leg up to get to his feast, Danburn ate her like he'd wanted to do it his entire life.

"Please. I'm going to fall." Her voice was weak, her body

trembling when he helped her to the ground. But as soon as she was there, he knew it was time to have her. Sliding up her body, he suckled at her breast until her legs came up around his hips and his cock was at her entrance.

"You belong to us. No one but us." She only stared up at him as his beast kept telling him to take her. "Tell me, Kendrick. Tell me you belong to us."

"I don't know what that means." He moved into her, the crown of his cock filling her the way he wanted his entire body to. "Please, take me."

"Say it. I need to hear you say it." She moaned when he moved in and out of her again. "Christ, I need you. I need you to tell me you belong to us."

"I belong to you and your dragon. Now take me." He filled her with his cock, and his heart too. As he took her, feeling her body accepting his and the dragon's, he knew that on some level there would be no turning back from this. And he didn't want to. When he cupped her ass to his body, pulling her clit and her pussy tightly against his groin, she screamed out his name, telling him over and over that she was theirs. Danburn felt his own climax take him, the beast within him coming as well. And when he leaned into her throat to make her his, his dragon took him a little and they both tasted their mate's blood.

Danburn held her to him as she lay limp beneath him. Rolling to his back, keeping her safely in his arms, he looked up at the wall of the castle that had brought them together. Because he had no doubt that without the stone's help, he would never have been able to explain to her what he was. Holding her with one hand, he dug his hand deep within the soil under them and thanked them.

*You are most welcome, my lord. She is the one and true, as you have guessed.* He had, but until now hadn't been sure. *The mountain and I have a gift for her if she would accept it from you. It has been within us since long before you woke us to work with you.*

*I cannot know the mind of her. Whether she will or will not accept your gift will be up to her.* The earth said that it understood and he felt something fill his hand. Before he pulled it from the earth, he asked it about her ability to talk to them.

*Nay, it was not the bullet as she believes. It did awaken that part of her, but it was there, all along, for her to use should she need it. I think she relaxed enough after her injury to allow us to speak as you and I do now.* He said he didn't understand that. *When the mother shot the child, the bullet entered a place that should have killed her. But with the power, her power that was hidden there for her, it was not able to destroy what she was. Instead, it woke it. Bringing to life what she would need to find you.*

*You knew that she was meant for me.* The earth said that it knew a great many things he did not. *I am sure that you do. And I am humbled in that knowledge. But I am not sure that she is as easily convinced as I would hope she is.*

*You will never know unless you ask her. And I would, if I were you, ask from now on. With this claiming, she has more than she had before. And she can harm you.* He thought that the earth meant his heart and said as much. *Nay, not only your heart, my lord, but you as a person and dragon as well. She is stronger than even you believe her to be. But she wakes now. Talk to her and give her our gift, please. It will keep her safe even when you are not there to keep her in your arms.*

Danburn looked up at Kendrick, who was indeed awake. He could see the confusion in her eyes, as well as some embarrassment. He kissed the tip of her nose, thinking that it was as wonderful as the rest of her body, and felt the item from the earth move in his hand again.

"I have a gift for you." When she started to rise, he held her with his hand. "Please, not yet. It really isn't from me, but from the earth. She said that it's been beneath her for longer than I have been here."

"I don't need a gift." He had hurt her, and unlike the other time, he knew why. When she struggled to move again, he rolled her to her back and settled over her. "Please let me up. I don't need you to treat me like a whore."

"No, and I never meant to either. Do you believe me when I tell you what I am?" She didn't say anything. "You know about us, the dragon and me, and that we claimed you. Do you know what you've given us?"

"My all." He nodded, and she looked away from him. Asking her to look at him again, he was afraid that she'd not do it, but she finally relented. "I don't want you to pay me for this. I don't want you to cheapen it."

"I never thought to pay you, not for giving us such pleasure. As I have said, the earth has a gift for you. You already have everything that I have...I have nothing left to give you. But should you want something, I will find it for you." He watched her face as it heated. "You are beautiful when you are embarrassed. More than usual."

"What is this gift? And please don't lie to me. For some reason I can't make you tell me the truth, and I would appreciate it if you didn't lie." He told her that he'd never lie to her. "Everyone lies to me, Danburn. Unless I make them do otherwise."

"I will not lie to you. Not ever. I will not keep things from you either, which to me is the same thing." He pulled the gift from the earth. "This is from her, the lady of the earth. She asked that you accept it from her, please."

Danburn had a feeling he knew what it was even before

she picked it up from her chest and began to clean the grass and roots from it. Rolling to his back again, he sat her up on his lap and watched her. She was beautiful. She was his and his forever. When she held the ring in her hands, he smiled at her, taking it from her hand and slipping it on her finger.

The ring fit her like it had been made only for her, which he supposed it had. And the pink and white diamond that sat upon the stone band was as big as any he'd ever seen, and he'd bet more pure. Pulling her to him for a kiss, Danburn felt as if he'd just taken her as his wife, and he could not have been happier. But he thought he'd wait a while in telling her his feelings. Yes, it was by his own admission a lie, but one that would keep him from harm.

# *Chapter 6*

Louisa wasn't sure what was going on, but she was happy with the results. People were doing what she wanted them to and she didn't have to keep asking them for it. Plus, her sister was coming to see her today. And while she was here, Louisa was going to tell her what those men wanted who had shot her and see how she was going to fix it for her. This time, Louisa was going to be good, she'd tell her.

It was hard to do with all the things she wanted to try yet. Louisa was still a little hurt at Kendrick for not helping their mother when she'd been out of work and living under the bridge for so long. But Kendrick had told her that their mother had tried to kill her, and that she was dead as far as she was concerned.

"But she's not."

Kendrick had said nothing but continued to refuse to help her. So Louisa had done her best to get her mom things that she wanted. Mostly it had been food, but there were times when she'd had to get her drugs too, and that was when Louisa would get herself into trouble again. Then her mom had died.

She had to admit that things were easier since her mom had passed away. Going to look for her all the time was the reason she'd had to have Kendrick bail her out of jail a couple of times. Her mom would get into places that weren't safe, and Louisa would have to stay with her to make sure that she wasn't hurt. The fights between them, she and her sister, had been terrible, and had left Louisa feeling like a part of her heart was beat up.

The nurses were really nice when they came in to give her things. Her meals were always nice, and there was plenty of food. The doctor answered her questions when she asked him. No one treated her like she was on welfare here, and they all seemed to go out of their way to get her whatever she wanted, so long as it didn't interfere with their work or her getting better. That had been the hardest part to remember for her, not to get in their way when they were busy. When she was alone, however, she thought of what she'd seen.

Someone had told her about the castle way back off the road, and she had decided to go and see it for herself. It had only taken her an hour to walk to where she thought it was supposed to be. But she'd gotten turned around again, and had lost her way. When she'd come out of the woods she could see the castle, and had started that way when she heard the shouts.

Louisa thought they were yelling at her at first. She'd slipped back into the woods to run when she saw the men. A lot of them were standing around with guns and rifles, so she moved deeper into the wooded area, but stayed where she could still see what was going on. The man who seemed to be in charge was yelling at some guy that was tied to a tree, and telling him how disappointed he was in him.

"All this time, here you were stealing from me." The man said that he hadn't been. He didn't know where the drugs had come from. "They came from my stash. That's where you got them from. Right, August? And now look at what I have to do. I have to take time out of my busy day, making all these workers come here and watch you hang yourself because you can't live with the fact that you bit the hand that feeds you. This will be a lesson for them too. Not to steal from me no matter what."

"I didn't do it, Mr. Bullock. I swear it." The rope around the man's neck was thick. But the stool under him was nice and sturdy, so she thought he was safe from falling. Louisa had no idea what the man in the suit was talking about. August didn't look to her like he wanted to kill himself at all. When he spoke again, she wanted to tell Mr. Bullock to listen to the man, that he might need some help. "Please, Mr. Bullock, I swear to you I never stole from anyone in my life."

As she watched with the rest of the men who looked to her like they'd rather be anywhere but there, Mr. Bullock kicked the stool out from under August. As he hung there, his face getting darker and darker, she wanted to go and save him, but nearly wet her panties when a man was suddenly in front of her. One of the men with a gun.

"Hello, Louisa."

The small scream startled them both. Louisa left behind her nightmares and looked at her sister, frightened. Reaching out to pull Kendrick to her for a much needed hug, Louisa started telling her what had happened to have gotten her shot, babbling much too fast for Kendrick to understand her. She asked her to slow down and think as she told her. Kendrick was here now and she'd be safe.

"You were shot, the doctors said. When did that happen? Was it the man you were talking about, this Bullock person?" Louisa wasn't sure she cared for the big man with Kendrick. He was bossy and seemed to think that everyone was his underling. "Then you ended up in my lake."

"Your lake? No one owns a lake, silly." He said nothing but looked at her. "I went there to look at the castle. I suppose you're going to tell me that it belongs to you too."

"It does, as a matter of fact. My mother and I live there, and now so does Kendrick. But you didn't answer me about who shot you. Was it Bullock or one of his men?" Louisa looked at her sister, wanting her to deny it, but she was looking at the man. That was when she noticed how her sister was dressed.

"You win the lotto? I mean, wow, those are pretty clothes. I got mine all wet, so I'm going to need some more. Do you have any extra money I can have?" Kendrick said she'd talk to her about it later. "I want to be pretty like you, Kendrick. I'm betting you have a little extra. There is this new shop on Twelfth that has some pretty things like you have on. I'd like those to wear. Nice things like you have on."

"I don't have anything, Louisa. In the event you've forgotten, you took all my money when you broke into my home again. What about this man, this Mr. Bullock? You said that he killed August. What happened after that?" Louisa wanted to talk about the clothing, but her sister was right. The more information she had, the quicker she could make it so she could get some pretty things. "When were you shot the first time?"

"I was running. He tried to shoot me when he came up on me, but his gun was jammed up or something. So I ran at him, then took off toward where I'd seen the castle. It's really nice too. You should see it…well, I guess you did see it if you're living there. Can I go and stay there too? It'll be really cool to tell my friends I live in a castle now." Kendrick cleared her throat. "Oh yeah, the man. He shot at me one time and it buzzed by my head. Then one of them hit me in the arm here. After that, I wasn't sure if he was still shooting at me or if I was getting hurt running. I found the pretty lake just about when I figured out that I couldn't run anymore. All my things got ruined in the water when I jumped in. When can you get me things to wear, Kendrick? I want pink, not green like you have on. And the castle. I want to see where I'm going to be living in the castle too."

"How long did they chase you?" She wanted to tell the man that there were more important things to talk about than the men who were no longer here, but he asked her again and again until she finally had to think.

Louisa thought about how long it felt like she had run. Tree branches had hit her in the face so many times she'd felt like it was raw. And she'd fallen a lot too. Mostly at the end… that was when she thought she might die.

"I remembered I had that phone you gave me and I called you. I don't know why you didn't come right then and get me. I did tell you I was in trouble. I even told you that some men were coming after me. When I'm at the castle, will I have my own room or will I have to share it with you? It looked really big, so I'm betting I can have my own place, right?" She glared at Kendrick when she thought of how her sister had not been there for her. "You've been doing that a lot lately. Not coming to help me."

"I was working four jobs to pay my bills and dig you out of any trouble you got into. Every time you came by my place, you'd find my stash and take it. It mattered little to you that it was my rent money or my food money. I got my electric shut off too." Louisa told her she was sorry and asked about the clothing again. "I don't have the funds to get you anything right now. And you're always sorry after you do it, Louisa. But that doesn't help me when I have nothing to pay my bills with."

"I try really hard to make things work for me. I had a job too, but I kept messing up remembering when I had to be there. And when I wrote it down, that guy there would change it around on me, so I'd end up being late or something." She glanced at the man, then looked at Kendrick again. "I don't know why you never let me just live with you. I wouldn't have to be on the streets where I get into trouble all the time. Once we're in the castle together, you can set me up with an account of my own and I won't have to bother you so much for things. You'll have to make sure there is always money in it though. I know how you hate to be bothered about money."

"Perhaps if you got yourself a job and worked at it, you'd not be in trouble either. You seem like a reasonably intelligent woman. Why not get yourself together and stop thinking people are going to bail you out all the time?" Louisa wasn't sure, but she thought maybe he'd just insulted her. "And you are not coming to live with us. Not in the castle or any of the property surrounding it."

"Why not? I saw the place, and it's big enough for all of us. Kendrick, tell him that I have to live there. It's like a dream come true for me." Kendrick looked at her. "Tell him that you have to take care of me. You have been all my life, and I don't want you to stop doing it now. And as soon as I have some pretty things, I'll be just as happy as I can be."

"There won't be any money, no account set up for you, and no clothing that you don't need. You're not going to move into the castle, and you most certainly aren't going to be taking any more money from me. I'm done, Louisa. And the only reason I did it for so long was because I thought I had to. But I really don't. You can do this. I did. Just get out and make it work for you. You've caused me enough trouble over the years." Louisa thought she was kidding with her. It was the same speech she'd given her time and time again. "I'm not going to do this anymore, Louisa. You have to stand up on your own two feet."

"But I'm hurt. And we're going to live together in that big castle, the three of us." Her sister said nothing, and Louisa didn't even bother looking at Danburn. He was the cause of this. "I'm guessing you think you want to impress this guy and all because he let you sleep in his castle. Is that it, Kendrick? You think he's going to give you something and you don't want me to have it? That's not too fair of you. Mom always said men only had one thing in mind and when they got it, they'd toss you aside. If there isn't enough money for me, I'm sure I can find someone to buy some of his things. When I move in with you, I can figure that all out."

"He's asked me to marry him." Louisa looked at Danburn and snorted. There was no way this man wanted to marry her sister. "And I'm going to."

"He asked, he didn't do it. And we both know that he's too good for you. Look at him. I bet his suit alone cost more than your old place did. And we both know that your stuff, when you had it, wasn't all that good." Louisa glanced at Danburn when he stood up. "Just look at him, Kendrick. He's not for you. He's too much. And when he's done with you, he's going to toss you out on your butt, and then you'll need me."

"I'm not going to toss her out anywhere. Have you always been this negative to people who try to help you?" She asked him what he thought Kendrick had done for her lately. Or him, for that matter. "Who do you think is putting you up in this private room, catering to your every need? You're only here and getting this good of care because Kendrick is your sister and I'm going to marry her."

"If she had come to me when I told her I needed her to, then I'd not be hurt in the first place. This is all her fault anyway." He looked at her, shocked, but Louisa was telling him like it was. "Listen, Kendrick. When I move in the castle with you, I'll take care of you so that he won't send us packing without any money. I swear to you, every day I get hurt or something happens to me. Once we're all living together, things will be better, don't you think? Living in the castle is going to be so cool. My parties are going to be epic. Mom would have loved it too, living up there in that big monster place. She'd be here if you hadn't just abandoned her."

"Abandoned her? You mean like she did after shooting me in the head? When she left me there to die? You mean like that?" Louisa tried again to tell her that she'd been hungry and needed a place to live. "And what if she had shot you, Louisa? Would you have the same feelings for her had it been you lying on the floor bleeding to death?"

"You make it sound so serious. My goodness, Kendrick. You didn't die, did you? You got to hang out in a hospital all the time with a warm bed and food." She showed her the scar on her arm that she'd been using as a backup when Kendrick got all bossy with her. "You remember how I got this? When we were running from the law that got called on us when you were injured? I didn't have any warm bed like you did. I was running with our mom."

Kendrick came toward her and lifted her hair up. Louisa wasn't sure what she was doing until she saw the long scar along her head. It was wide, and no hair grew there. She backed from Kendrick when she grabbed her hand and put it on her head. Louisa jerked her hand back when she realized what it was and where it had come from.

"Do you feel that one, Louisa? The scar that I have from when you and Mother decided that instead of you being shot, it would be me?" Louisa told her she wasn't being fair. "I'm not being fair? How do you suppose that works?"

"Well, like I said, you didn't die, did you? I don't know what all this fuss is about anyway. I just wanted to tell you that I'm glad to see you. And when I get out of here, I promise you I will try my best not to steal from you again, and I won't let anyone come into your house and steal stuff. Not unless they want to hurt me again for money. You know that was the only reason I let them in to take your bed and couch." Louisa smiled at Kendrick when she just stood there. "Come on, you know you want to help me out. It's what we do. I get into trouble, you bail me out. We're sisters."

"I never realized until this very moment how selfish you are. And how...you really expect me to just let you keep doing this to me, stealing from me because of some sense of obligation because I'm your sister? What have you ever done for me?" Louisa asked her what she meant by that. "You know, you steal from me, make me behind in everything, including eating, and what have you ever done for me?"

"Kendrick, I think you're making a big deal out of nothing. Are you trying to impress this guy?" She laughed. "It's not necessary. He already said that you could live in his castle with him. And you won't want me not to have the same kind of fun. Besides, he's not going to last and when he's done, you and I are going to go back to the way we were before. You have to take care of me. We're sisters."

"Why? Why am I responsible for anything you do? Yes, we're sisters, but that doesn't mean I'm going to let you continue doing to me what you are. I'm done. Finished." Louisa told her again that they were sisters, not understanding why she didn't get that. "And that is supposed to be reason enough for me to continue to be hungry and poor all the time."

"I'm not responsible for you being hungry. And if you're poor, maybe you shouldn't be spending your money on new clothing and stuff." She looked at the sweater and new jeans that Kendrick had on. "I could really use something like that to wear. I need it. When you go and get them for me, I would like mine to be prettier. Okay? That way when we're in the castle together, people at my parties will know how much you care for me."

Kendrick said nothing. She sat down in the room's only chair when Danburn went to stand by the window. He was pissed off, Louisa could tell, but he wasn't really important to her. Nor was he important to her sister. Men, especially men like this one, would only want to hang onto Kendrick until someone new and shiny came along. And even as nice as she looked right now, Kendrick wasn't really all that shiny. Louisa decided that she'd have a talk with her when the man wasn't around. She might be able to sell some things of his to use when he kicked her out. It wasn't really stealing from him, like Kendrick kept saying, but making sure that she had what she needed in an emergency. Louisa thought she could do well with some things this guy might have laying around his big castle to make herself a nice little place for a while.

But when Kendrick just left her, got up without saying a word and left the room, Louisa wondered what had happened. Looking at Danburn, she knew that she'd get no answers from him and lay back on the bed. When he left too, Louisa felt better. Things would work out as they always did for her. Kendrick would do the right thing by her. She was her sister, after all.

~~~

The cool air felt good on her face. Kendrick turned her face up, feeling the breeze as it blew over her, making her feel like she was getting all the cruelty of her sister blown off her. She knew it was Danburn when a shadow moved over her.

"I never realized until this minute what kind of person she is. And what a monster I created by doing things for her." He didn't say anything, and she wondered if he was mad at her. It wouldn't surprise her if he was. "I can't deal with her right now. I'll take care of her when I can, but for now, I just need to breathe."

"I'm going to have my attorney give her some money and a place to stay. She can have a couple of months of living there for free before I will…we will expect her to get a job and try to get her shit together. You were right in calling her selfish. She is by far one of the most selfish, self-centered people I know." He put his hands on her arms and turned her toward him. When she looked into his eyes, she felt her heart break for what had happened in there. "You didn't do this to her, Kendrick. Yes, she's your sister, but you in no way made her like she is right now."

She laid her head on his chest. It was warm and she needed to feel something other than pain and the coldness of her sister's words right now. Kendrick thought of all the things that Danburn had told her this morning. Things about him and his mother. How old he was and how much he was worth. Then he'd asked her to marry him, to be his wife.

Kendrick wasn't sure that she loved Danburn. If she was honest with herself, she wasn't even sure what love was. She'd not felt anything for her sister for a long time but annoyance. Her mother had been dead to her after she'd shot her all those years ago. And the few men that had been in her life, mostly losers needing more from her than just her heart, she had never felt anything for. But this man, he did make her feel something.

"She just doesn't think she's done anything wrong. That everything she's done, it's justified because she wanted it and that I'm to forgive her because we're related by blood." He said he got that. "I mean, she feels like just because I didn't die, that somehow means that I'm going to be there for her the rest of my life."

"She doesn't deserve you. And if we keep giving in to her, she's going to be doing this to us for the rest of her life. And long after she's gone, she'll be hurting you." She looked up at him, remembering what he'd said to her that morning. She would live forever now. "Let me take care of this for you. I'll do what you want, but I think that if you continue on the path you were on, she's going to keep getting into more trouble all the time. At some point, it's going to get you hurt. And I don't think I could handle that. I can't stand the thought of her hurting you anymore, love."

"Yes. I know that now. I mean, why not keep going on the path that she's on? There never seemed to be any consequences for her before this because I was always there to get her out of trouble. So why not just go about her merry way and do whatever the fuck she wants?" Kendrick still blamed herself for her sister's behavior. "I can't believe I let her do this to me all these years. And for nothing."

"No, it wasn't for nothing. You love her and she is your sister. But today, I think this is the first time...." He lifted her chin up and looked her in the eyes. "You never made her tell you the truth before, did you? You just took what she said to you as gospel, and she did what she wanted. Why today?"

"I don't know. I saw her looking at my new things, which I love by the way, and I felt like she was going to cheapen them. I have no idea why, but I wanted the truth from her. All of it, even if it hurt me." He asked her if it did. "Yes. But not in the way I thought it would. She hurt me because I realized then that I have never meant anything to her other than as someone she could depend on for money and other support. Love was never the reason for any of it."

"I think she loves you in her own way." Kendrick snorted at him. "Okay, she was a manipulative woman who rode you like the bitch she thought you were."

"Wow. Okay, that was a little over the top." She watched his face as he looked down at her with laughter in his eyes. "These men, you think they'll try and get to her still? I mean, you think she was telling the truth about them hanging that man, right? What do we do about that?"

"I'm looking into a few things. I have some friends in high places that I can have see what is going on out there." She asked him who, the president? "No. The lady of the earth. She will help if for no other reason than whatever they're doing there has got to be affecting her realm. I'll talk to her when I get back to the castle."

As they were riding back, she thought of her sister. There was something very sad about her. Not the kind of down on her luck sort of sad, but Kendrick thought that her sister had led a sad life until now. She'd never had to pay for things. Never had to work hard at making a life work for herself. If it didn't fit for her at that very moment, then she would move on and run to Kendrick. But no more. Kendrick was finished with being taken for granted.

"I'd like to handle my sister." Danburn didn't say anything but watched her. "I'm going to be the one to tell her what's going to happen and how it's going to work for her from now on. I know that it's a lot to ask of you, but if you can please do as you suggested, have a contract drawn up for her and let me have some money, I'll be able to...I need to be able to cut ties from her. Otherwise, like you said, her troubles are going to grow and grow, and she might pull me along with her."

"She will." Danburn nodded. "All right. If you want to do this, that's fine with me. But I would like for you to take Noah with you. Not because I don't think you can handle her, but because he could stand as your witness. He's done enough for me over the years, and I think he could be a steady force for you as well."

"You think she'll try to hurt me?" He said that she'd already done that. "Yes, but you think she'd do something physically to me? To hurt me to get what she wants? I don't know why, but I don't think she will. She needs me too much to let physical harm come to me."

"I think she will, honey. I think your sister is used to getting her own way and will stop at nothing to continue getting it. Even if it means bringing a shit load of hurt down on you if you don't cooperate. It's not your fault, not entirely, but enough is enough, don't you think?" She did and told him that. "I'll have my...our attorney draw up the paperwork today and you can set up a time to go over it with her. You can explain Noah being there as he can answer questions she might have. All right?"

"Yes. But you don't have to keep saying *our*. I don't have anything but what you want to give me." He pulled her onto his lap so quickly that she squeaked a little. "Danburn, I'm not stupid. I know that we have nothing in common and that you have more money than I'd ever hope to have."

"*We* have money. *We* have a castle and *we* have attorneys. Say it. *We*. I like the way it rolls off my tongue." He kissed her then, making her feel all wet and bothered at the same time. "Christ, I wish that I could lay you out here and take you. But I have to go to work. You need to go with my mom."

"Oh yeah." She was supposed to go to the mall with his mom. She was going to help her get more clothing, as well as a dress for this thing that Danburn had to attend over the weekend. "I could just wear these. They're very nice."

"They are very nice, but you need more things, pretty things that I love seeing you in. You deserve them." She still wasn't sure about that, but said nothing about it this time. The last time she'd mentioned it, he'd swatted her on the ass. It had been sexy as hell, but also a little painful. "And have fun. You deserve that more than you do anything. You've been without it for a long time."

She didn't know how much fun she was going to be able to have. Kendrick had never been to the mall for any other reason than to hand in a job application. She'd never bought herself anything that hadn't been marked down so much it was practically free. And her shoes were as old as some of the underwear that she'd had to toss when Danburn had gotten a look at it. He'd been very sexy holding up her clothing and then tossing them over his shoulder when she told him how old they were, but now she had nothing much to wear.

Kendrick was still getting used to having someone care about her. Now she had to go out and find clothing that would look good when she was with him. She wasn't looking forward to this at all.

# Chapter 7

Elissa watched Kendrick walk around the large shop. Any number of women were there to help her, once they found out who she was engaged to anyway. When they'd first entered, it was all she could do not to slap the piss right out of the woman behind the cash register. But the manager had come right out and fixed things. For now, anyway.

The woman had told Kendrick that she wasn't to touch anything she didn't plan on paying for. Elissa had been so shocked that she'd stood there for several seconds while the woman went on to tell Kendrick that things were there to buy, not to manhandle.

Elissa had nearly grabbed her up and taken her away when Kendrick had looked at the woman, pulled a dress off the hanger, and dropped it on the floor. Then she turned to Elissa with a smile on her face that did not bode well for the woman.

"Did Danburn tell me what sort of dress I needed for our

wedding? I wasn't sure if he said cheap, like they have here, or something more fitting for the queen of the castle." Then she looked at the bitch again. "You talk to me like that again and I will not only own this shop and everything in it, I will burn it in effigy, with your picture right here in the middle of this store."

Now they just stood back and only came toward her when she asked a question. Elissa was going to enjoy watching this woman grow into becoming the queen she claimed she was. And Elissa was looking forward to seeing the grandchildren that she gave her as well. But first things first.

"Perhaps you should just grab a few of them and try something on to see your size." Kendrick looked at her, and Elissa saw the fear there, and the embarrassment. "Come here, child. I think we need to take a break."

The restaurant was busy, but they were seated right away. She supposed that it was she that had gotten them to the front of the line and not the younger woman at her side. But that, too, would change, and Kendrick could command armies if need be. As soon as they sat down, Elissa ordered two iced teas and an appetizer to hold them over while they talked. Kendrick was overwhelmed, and it was showing on every part of her body.

"My husband was like you are right now. Scared and unsure of himself. He had Noah, of course, to help him when needed. But he wasn't really born to being rich. But he did love knowing that he was secure in it." She asked if he was going to join them. "No, sadly he passed away long ago. I still talk to him, go out to his grave and sit with him. Danburn had a lovely bench put out there, and the gardener put in some pretty flowers for me."

"I'm sorry. You must have loved him a great deal." Elissa

said she'd loved him with all that she was. "I never really cared for my mom. I mean, even before she shot me. My mom would steal for no other reason than someone had it. And then she'd break it so that no one else could have it either. Louisa was always the special one. I didn't really understand why until recently. She was a suck up."

Elissa laughed. "Yes, I can see that. Danburn told me about your visit with her. She wasn't all that supportive of you, he said."

"No. I don't think.... I'm pretty sure I knew she was like that all along, but I've come to realize that instead of seeing the problem, I gave her what she wanted. Well, let her take what she wanted rather than deal with her. She was always needy, clingy, and I would just want her to go away. I should have taken a better stand. I might have had a better life had I done something sooner. Do you understand?" Elissa nodded. She didn't think that would have worked either, but kept her mouth closed. "You and Danburn, you have a good relationship, don't you?"

"Yes. He's my only little boy." Kendrick smiled, just as she'd wanted her to. "He and I, we only had each other when his dad died. Even before that, the three of us were all we had. Fletcher, Danburn's father, was a good man, but had a hard time getting over the fact that I loved him and cared not where he came from. You know there are more of us out there, don't you? I mean, someday, soon I bet, you'll have visits from them too."

"I just want to get used to the two dragons I know right now, thanks. Noah told me that he thought that Danburn was a snob when he talked to him about me. I'm not sure what that conversation might have been like, but he said he was sorry for thinking the things that he had about me. I just thought

Danburn was an ass." The appetizers were set in front of them, and Elissa handed her part of it on a plate as she laughed. "He's so bossy all the time. I know that he's working on it, but there are times when I want to throat punch him."

"Yes, well, I would refrain from that. He'd never hit you back, but he might be hurt. Dragons have a different body frame than humans. Danburn's dragon's heart is close to his throat." Kendrick nodded, and Elissa was glad to realize that Danburn had told her a few things about himself. "But back to my husband. When I met him, he had less than you did when you met Danburn. A great deal less."

"I don't know how that's possible. I had nothing and owed out more than I'd ever be able to pay. I'm sorry. That sounded crass. Danburn said that his dad was a great man. What did he do for a living?" She told him he was a cinder man. "I'm sorry. I thought, well, I thought he was like you and Danburn, a dragon."

"He was. That was what made him so successful as a cinder merchant." Kendrick looked like she was going to ask why, then smiled. "I see you get it. He could have fresh cinders whenever he wanted. But like I said, he was like you when it came to his station in life."

"You mean poor." Elissa nodded. "I could have been something, I think. I mean, I know that I could have. I had a scholarship when I graduated from high school. It wasn't much, but it would have given me a hand up. But my sister...I let her mess up a great many things in my life that I've come to regret. Mostly, it was just my life. Your husband...did he get used to having money? Spending it on things that he wanted? I'm not sure how I'll get used to that either."

"You were some at fault, but not all. You had no support system in place. None that would help you. And yes, he did eventually get into spending money. Mostly on Danburn and I, and he so enjoyed the holidays. When we all moved into the castle together, he made it his mission to fill it with things that no one else would think to have. Tapestries from all over the world. Art and pottery that he admired. He even bought the first lamp we have in the house, when electricity was invented for the masses." She leaned back when the plate was empty. "My husband loved life. Not when I met him, but after we came to be one. It was…difficult at the beginning. He'd been walking the neighborhood when I could smell what he was. It took me days to find him. From the fires that he would light with his magic, his scent would linger for days after he was gone. I'd follow his scent for days before I'd come to realize that he hadn't been there for hours. But when I found him, it broke my heart to see what someone had done to him."

Elissa thought of her giant of a husband. Not in stature, but in heart. He'd been trying to get enough coin to eat. He'd been digging in trash heaps for a long time and had only wanted to have a good meal, he'd told her, one that had been prepared for him and not leftovers. She thought she might have fallen in love with him then.

"He'd been beaten, again. Apparently, this happened to him a great deal. I helped him to stand, only to have to carry him nearly all the way back to my home. My family had left years before, to find a quieter, a more…I guess you would say accepting place to live." Kendrick asked her if they had found it. "Nay, sadly, they only met with their deaths. I'm not sure, but there were times when it first happened that I thought they had left me so they could die in peace and with each other. My parents were old, set in their ways, but they had good hearts. They were just closed off to change."

The waiter brought them menus, and they both ordered.

Elissa was glad to see that Kendrick ordered a big meal, not one of those kinds that only a bird could live off of. She grinned at her after he left them.

"I feel hungry all the time now." Elissa nodded but didn't mention why. Danburn was keeping her very active, she'd bet. "Danburn said that he burns a lot of calories just sitting around. Which I doubt he does all that often."

"No, he likes to keep busy." She asked what happened to Fletcher when he got to her home. "He healed for the most part. He was never very healthy. I think it had to do with his upbringing, the way that he had to live to survive. But we were happy. We loved each other very much. Then we had Danburn and our life seemed to be complete."

"That's a wonderful story with such a happy ending. I hope someday.... I don't love him. Danburn, I mean. I like him most of the time." Her face turned a deep red as she continued. "He makes me feel good about myself, and while he's still really bossy at times, I like talking to him about his day. He doesn't treat me like he did at first. More like his equal, though I don't know why he'd think that."

"You are his equal, love. In all ways. Do you plan to work?" She said that she had to. "No, you really don't. I mean, I know that you've been told that there is plenty of money."

"I don't mean to sound ungrateful for the money. I've figured out over the last few days that it's really nice having beautiful things. But I don't want to feel like I have to ask for every penny I want to spend." Elissa asked if Danburn had told her she had to. "No. But I still feel that I need to ask. It's really not my money no matter how many times he's told me it's ours. I mean, he's very nice to make it so I have pretty things. But I do need to be able to stand on my own two feet. And he has asked me to marry him. I've not answered him yet, not really, but I can't think that this will work out for us. Do you?"

"And why not?" Elissa was very proud of the girl for wanting to work. She was impressed that she'd not just said yes to marrying her son right away, but thought about it first. She wanted her to, more than she could have ever thought, but she loved that she wasn't just blindly stepping into something that would change her life forever. "I've explained that coming from different classes works out, haven't I?"

"You explained to me that you and your husband worked it out. Whatever happens between Danburn and me isn't like you and your husband. Danburn is…he's very set in his ways, isn't he? I mean, he is trying to be different, but I don't want to be ruled any more than I'd bet you would." She told her to stand up to him. "Oh, I have no problem doing that. Just today he and I had a terrible fight about the credit cards that he wanted me to have."

"I heard." Elissa laughed when Kendrick turned red again. "I think, and this is just me, but I think he argues with you just to see you get upset."

"That's insane. Why would he want me to be pissy with him?" Elissa could see the moment that she got it. "Oh. Make up sex. That doesn't make it any less insane."

"No, but it's funny to me." When their salads came, Kendrick played with hers. There was more to this than just him pissing her off, and Elissa waited. "Did you know that once we get done shopping here, we're to go and get our hair done?"

"Great. Another thing I'm not going to be any good at." Before Elissa could ask her what she meant, Kendrick continued. "They're going to ask me what I want, or who cut my hair before. It was me. I chopped my hair when it no longer stayed in a ponytail. And as for color? I have no idea what color my hair is. Black? No. Is it brown? Who the hell knows? And don't even get me started on wearing makeup. I could never afford it even if I had any idea how to smear it all over my face."

It took all Elissa had not to laugh. The girl was honest to a fault; she'd say that for her. As she cut up her lettuce, all the while keeping an eye on Kendrick stabbing at the tomatoes like she had a vision of some monster in mind, Elissa tried to think what to say. Then she thought, what the hell. Honesty deserves honesty.

"No one will say a word about who has cut your hair. They're going to be too amazed that you're Danburn's future wife and that they get you in their chair to care if you have bright blue hair or orange. I have no idea what color your hair is either, and see no reason for you to care what they think. It's pretty, leave it at that. Makeup?" She did laugh a little then. "I don't think you want to begin smearing it on your face this late in the game. You have a beautiful fresh look about you, and I heard Danburn remark to Noah that he loved the way you looked when you got up in the morning. I think there might have been something about smell too, but I didn't catch it all."

"I've been using his crap in the shower. So if I smell, it's his fault." Elissa added another shop to her list of places to go. As they both ate, she wondered aloud if Kendrick wanted to change anything in the castle. "Change? You mean like furniture or something? No. I love it just the way it is. It's beautiful and homey. I've never lived in...well, I don't know many people who have lived in a castle, but I bet those that have would love it too. I think everything about it is perfect. Just the way one would imagine a castle to look."

Their lunches arrived, and Elissa could see that Kendrick was much more relaxed. She hated to bring it up now, but they had a lot to do before they could head back home. Before she could mention it however, Kendrick spoke.

"I don't know how to buy clothing that doesn't have a clearance tag on it. I know nothing of brand names or matching outfits. The only pair of heels I've ever worn was at a job interview where I ended up taking one of them off to hit the guy with it." Elissa told her she might not want to mention that part to Danburn. "Yeah, I got that he has a jealous streak going. Though I have no idea why. I'm surprised that he wants me, much less that other men do. Anyway, that lady in the store, she doesn't trust me and I know it. And the staff there smell like dogs."

"One of them is a wolf, not a dog." Kendrick didn't even raise her head from her food when Elissa explained how she knew that. "To be honest with you, I never liked the place either. It's always seemed to be over priced cheap crap. How about I take you where I shop?"

"Yes." The way she said it made Elissa think that she might have said yes to anywhere but the one shop they'd been in. "And if you don't mind, I'd really like to just get some jeans and some tee-shirts. I know that Danburn is all fancy and stuff, but I can't dress up all the time. I can't breathe."

"I understand completely. And if you can get him in a pair of jeans and shirt, I'll be forever indebted to you." Kendrick told her not to expect miracles.

Elissa decided that she loved this woman and was going to enjoy watching her tame her son. Because there was no doubt in her at all that Danburn would be eating out of her hand in no time.

~~~

Bernie wanted to pull out his gun and shoot the fucker right where he stood. The nerve of him coming here and accusing him of trying to murder a young woman. Bernie had ordered it done, but this guy had no proof of it. He didn't even glance in the direction of Collier. The man was as good as dead if this went badly. And he'd leave him out to rot in the sun too.

"You can understand our concern when someone ends up in the hospital with multiple gunshot wounds, and claims that she received them when she saw you kick the stool out from under one of your men." Bernie nodded, trying his best to keep his hands steady behind his back. If he moved them to the front of his body, the man was going to be dead. Officer Jake Ludlow would be no more. "She's told us what she allegedly saw several times now, and her story hasn't changed. I'm just here as a courtesy call to see what you can tell us about it."

"I don't know what to tell you, Officer Ludlow. We have a good crew here. Men working on the tree lines even as we speak." He had no idea what the lawyers had told the bigwigs about what he used this property for when he'd gotten them to buy it for him. He was sure they'd not said it was making drugs. "We have had some issues over the last several weeks, as you know, and we have cooperated with you on all of that. But men...I guess unlike me, they just can't stand to be away from their families for long periods of time."

"You have cooperated, yes. And that's why I'm here as a courtesy and not with a search warrant. For the moment anyway. She said she saw some things that led her to believe that you murdered a man for stealing your stash of drugs." Bernie shook his head. When he got ahold of this woman, he was going to show her what it looked like to have someone murdered. "What can you tell me about this man named

August?"

"August? I'm not sure if we have someone by that name here. Do you know if that's a first name or last?" He knew, as surely as he was standing here, that it was the man's first name. Not that he'd be using it again. The man was currently rotting away in the bottom of a deep pit they'd found on the property. And when the body count got too high in that one, he'd just have some of the schmucks that worked here dig another one. "I can have my secretary look into that for you and let your office know if you want. I can have her call you right away with what she finds."

"No, that won't be necessary. I can wait." *Of course you can*, he thought. *Anything to fuck up my day*. "While this person is looking for it, maybe you can give me a little tour of what you're doing here. I heard you were line running. I've never heard of cutting trees called that before."

Neither had he, but Bernie left him for a moment to go and call his secretary. She said August was the man that he'd had her delete from the system three days ago. Bernie counted to ten before he spoke to Angel, his niece, again.

"I know that and you know that, but I really don't want the police to find that information out. It will go badly for all of us if they find out that we have a few dead men laying around that we've not told them about." She said she got it now. "And I want you to find out all you can about someone being admitted to the hospital with multiple gunshot wounds. A female."

"Do you know her name?" Bernie counted to twenty this time as she continued talking. "It would make it easier if I had a name to work with. Those hospitals, they're getting very stingy with their information since the hippo law."

"Hippo? You mean HIPAA? It's the Health Insurance

Portability and Accountability Act, not an animal that lives in the fucking mud. And no, I don't know her name. That's why I'm having you look for information on her." Mother fuck, his head hurt every time he talked to her. The next time he thought to hire his sister's kids, he was going to shoot them all and be done with it. "If anyone asks about August Winehammer, what are you going to tell them?"

"Who?" He was going to kill her. "Oh, the man that you had me delete. I'm going to tell them that we don't have anyone working here by that name. Which I guess is true since you had me take him out of the comp—"

He hung up the phone. There was no way he could continue talking to her and not kill her. Bernie was going to have to keep them away from his offices, because he was sure she'd give him up and then think it was fucking funny when he was carted off to prison.

As he made his way back into the offices, he noticed that the cop was gone and asked Collier about it.

"He's using the john. I don't think he believes us." Bernie thought, just for a moment, that it might be worth going to prison for just to have the knowledge that he'd killed a lot of stupid people before going there. "What I mean is, I think that woman got a better look at us than Sams let on. There is no telling what other shit she got a look at."

He had to think who Sams was...the second guy that had died by his hand on the day the woman was watching. He'd let her get away, and didn't do anything about the bodies that were found. Instead of coming to him with what had happened, he'd gone home and packed his things to leave. The other shitball that had been with him when his men drowned was under his body in the pit as well. Fuckers. Bernie hated incompetent people.

"I thought he told us she was dead. Drowned like the other two idiots he had with him." There was no way he could go back and ask him to verify his story now. It was really too late for a lot of the things that had gone down that day. "Do you suppose that they've been able to trace those two to working here? It's not like we have uniforms or anything to make us look like we're on the same fucking team."

"No. We took off all the IDs and shit before we left them there. Good thing, too, because the police were hot on it. When they drove by us right after it happened, I thought for sure that we were caught. Who knew a missed turn could be so fucking inconvenient? We did miss one of the walkies, but I think it's at the bottom of that lake, and there isn't any reason for them to go looking for it." Bernie didn't think so either, but this shit was getting too real for him at the moment. Nothing to attach those two to what they did here. Until the woman, that is.

"She has to go." Collier nodded. But before either of them could plan how that was going to happen, the cop came back out of the bathroom.

"Well, I'm ready." Both he and Collier looked at each other, then back at Ludlow. "For the tour. It states in your contract with the state that I can drop by for a tour of the place when I want, so long as I don't become a nuisance. Since I've never requested one before, I can assume that I'm not. A nuisance, I mean."

"Well, you see, we're closing up for the day." He had no idea if they were working or not. That was not part of what he did here. He enforced and collected the money. A great deal of it, as a matter of fact. "I'm sorry about that. You'll just have to —"

"Earlier you said they were all working. That you have a good crew and that everyone was working today." Did he?

He had no fucking idea. "So, if you're ready, I'm ready."

He reached for his gun. There wasn't any help for it. The fucker had to go.

Just as he touched the gun at his back, the radio squawked on Ludlow's shoulder. He didn't so much as twitch his fingers when Ludlow answered the thing and stared him in the eye. He knew, Bernie's mind looped over and over, he knew he was about to be killed.

When Ludlow finished with the call, he rocked back on his heels and smiled at him. "Well, gotta go for now. Bad timing for us both, I guess." Bernie nodded at him, slowly moving his finger away from the gun and his hand down his back. "But you can be assured that I'll return, and when I do, I'll expect that tour."

"Of course."

As they followed him out to his car, Bernie wondered if he could find him a cop on the inside, someone at the station. He should have thought of it sooner, now that he thought on it. Everywhere else he'd been he'd had him a guy he could count on to give him a heads up when he needed it. As the cruiser pulled out of the lot, he looked over at Collier.

"Find out what you can about our police department here. Find me a man on the inside that I can depend on." Collier nodded. "And Angel needs to go. If I find out that you put her in the pit with those other pieces of shit, I'll toss your ass there too."

"Right. And the woman? What do you want done about her? I'm not sure where she is, but it won't be any problem finding her in this town." Bernie didn't think so either, but this had been fucked up for a while now. "I have a couple of people at the hospital. I'll start looking there."

"Find her, bring her here. I have no idea, but I think she

might be worth more to us alive than dead." Collier nodded and started to turn away when Bernie called him back. "Anyone else shows up here unannounced, you will never see the next sunrise. Do you hear me?"

"Yeah, I do."

As Collier moved away, Bernie stood looking at the top of the castle that butted up against his land. He wanted that place. Not just for his own home, but for the simple reason that the man who owned it had fought him so hard over this property. He had to get to him too.

Danburn English was, by all accounts, a very wealthy man. And he was powerful. When Bernie had been inquiring about a few empty buildings in town, he'd been told that he'd have to make arrangements with English, that English was the one who owned them. Twice more he'd asked about a hotel that was there, small and insignificant and perfect for any man coming in to settle up with him, but he'd been told that English used it for his own guests, that no one stayed there except people he approved of. The man was unknowingly becoming a pain in his ass. And it was about time that the two of them got together and buried the hatchet.

"Perhaps in his heart, if he has one."

Chuckling, he walked away. He had a shipment going out tonight, and he wanted to make sure that his men were aware of the fact that if there was one single fuck up, they'd all be dead. He wasn't above going out and recruiting more people to come and work for him. He'd get a crew yet he could depend on.

# *Chapter 8*

"Are you paying attention to me?" Kendrick wanted to shake her sister. She'd been wandering around the apartment for the last twenty minutes, and Kendrick wanted to be gone. She glanced over at Noah, who had not said a single word since they'd brought Louisa here over an hour ago when she'd been released from the hospital. "Louisa, you have to sit down and listen to what I'm telling you. In a few months, this will all be gone if you don't abide by the rules here in this contract."

"The things here, they're really nice, but it's so small, don't you think? I mean the apartment, not the furniture. It's all normal sized, isn't it?" Kendrick told her all of it was normal sized. "No, it's not. You have a nice big place at the castle, I bet. Oh, I get it. Is this just a place for me to stay until you get ready for me at the castle? I can stay in just about any room. When you set me up, make sure I have a nice pretty view."

"You're not going to be living in the castle. I've told you that several times now. You're not living there because you're living here. You can only stay here for six months if you don't get a job. All your utilities, as well as your phone, will be paid up until then. After that—"

"I come and live with you. Why didn't you just say that in the first place instead of all this other stuff? You want me to live here until you can get ready for me. Kendrick, you are always making things so hard. When do you think you're going to be ready for me? Soon? Like tomorrow?" *Yes*, Kendrick thought, *I'm going to slap my sister*. "It's going to be fun there. When I move in the castle, can I still come here if I want? I might have a boyfriend or something."

"Christ, Louisa. You're not going to live in the castle. Period. I don't know how else to make you understand that." Louisa pouted, putting out her lower lip so far that Kendrick thought she'd trip over it if she took a step. When she sat down again, Kendrick knew it was too much to hope that she was going to listen to her. "Now, back to this contract. You have six months to find a job and work at it. In that time, you'll have spending money and—"

"How much? I'm going to have me a party here, and that'll cost some money. I have to let my friends know where I am. And let them know that I'm going to be moving soon. You never told me when I was moving in with you." Kendrick shook her head, telling her there was going to be no party. "But why not? I bet you'll be having parties up there before I get to stay there. I just want to show off, Kendrick. Don't be a stick in the mud."

"I'm trying to make it so you can live, Louisa. Without having to end up like Mom did. Under a bridge somewhere." Louisa laughed and told Kendrick that she'd never let that happen to her. "I'm helping you now. If you don't do as this contract says, then I'm washing my hands of you."

"You're so serious. Don't be like that. Life is too short for you to be sounding so serious all the time." Louisa laughed again. "I know, and so do you, that my life is just fine the way it is. Because I have you. I just want to be happy, and that's all. Living here will be really nice and all, but I want to live up there with you. In the castle. Can you imagine what kinds of parties I can have up there?"

"There will not be any parties given by you, because you are never going to live there. Never, Louisa. I'm not going to be sucked into your life like this again. You've used me up." Louisa waved her off. "At the end of six months, if you don't have a job and keep it, all this will be gone. And I'm not going to bail you out, either."

"Yes you will. You always say that, but you always do. It's what sisters do for each other. And there won't be any need for this contract and six months of whatever, I'm going to be right there by your side in the big castle. Maybe we can come live here again when he's tired of you. He can afford it." Kendrick felt the tears again. Louisa had made her cry earlier when she'd told Kendrick that Danburn was never going to love her, that she wasn't loveable. "We're all we have, each other. Especially since you left Mom out there to die."

"That is quite enough, young lady." Both she and Louisa looked at Noah when he spoke. "You will read this over now and be quick about it. There will be no more pushing your sister into things either. This is all you will receive in the way of help, and if you mess this up, then it will be because you didn't take the time to try and better yourself."

"I don't need you telling me what to do. Besides, who are you anyway? Some flunky that does what the jerk told you to do? This is me and my sister talking. You stay out of it." Kendrick stood up and so did Louisa. "Are we leaving now?

Going to the castle?"

"Sign this, Louisa, or you're out on the street as of right now." Louisa stood there and glared at her, but she picked up the pen and signed her name where she was told. "Now, Noah has your money for this month, and when it's gone, that is all there will be. It's more money than I was ever able to give you before, and if you spend it right, you can live off of it."

Louisa squealed as she counted out the money. Then she looked at Kendrick. She could see her mind working out ways to spend it, and Kendrick would bet by the end of the day her sister would be broke, with nothing to show for it.

"When do I get the rest of it?" Kendrick told her next month. "But if I need more, you can get it to me, right? I'm sure he's paying you pretty good to sleep with him. I might run a little short and you'd hate that. When I move in with you, you'll make sure I have plenty of money too, won't you?"

"That's all there will be for thirty days. Spend it wisely." Louisa nodded and smiled. "All right. You have everything you need and enough food for a couple of weeks. If you find a job right away, let Noah know. He knows how to get in touch with me."

Noah had told her to let him handle any calls from Louisa. She had wanted to tell him she'd do it, but right now she was very glad that she'd agreed with him. Kendrick would bet that even before she got down the road Louisa would be calling, asking about the castle.

Louisa wasn't stupid…she really wasn't, but until the last few days, Kendrick had never realized how single minded she was. Manipulative really. And Kendrick was sure that was the reason she had given Louisa whatever she asked for. It was Louisa's sheer determination to have it that had worn Kendrick down over the years.

As they moved toward the door, Louisa stopped her.

"What's your phone number? I bet you have one of those fancy phones, huh?" Kendrick said nothing. "How am I supposed to call you to find out the arrangements for me to move into the castle with you? Because we both know that this guy isn't going to give you any messages from me. I need to talk to you. You're my sister, aren't you?"

"I am. But you're nearly thirty-five years old, and it's about time you stood up on your own two feet. I'm finished with all the drama of your life and you wanting me to fix everything. Figure it out on your own from now on." She asked her again what her number was, as if Kendrick had not said a single word. "Call Noah if you have a question about something. I have to get my life together, and I'll be too busy to talk to you all the time."

"Then I'll just come there." They had anticipated her saying that, and Kendrick told her that Danburn's security would keep her off the property. "That's not fair, Kendrick. You get to be there. Why not me too? I'm your sister. I have just as much right to be there as you do."

"Yes, you are my sister. My older sister who has been living off me for most of her life. I'm done, as I have said to you several times. You have to make your own way in this world. I can't always be there for you."

"You know you won't let me suffer. You never have." Kendrick said nothing as they made their way out to the limo that had brought them there. "Oh, that's really nice. Do I get one of those too? I would love to go to the grocery store in one of those. Can you imagine what people will say? When does mine get here? Or are we sharing that one? Kendrick?"

"Goodbye, Louisa. Get a job and a life that gives you what you want." Louisa told Kendrick that she'd given her all she wanted, and Louisa liked it that way. "But I'm not now. Goodbye."

As the limo pulled away, Louisa waved at them with a huge smile on her face. Noah handed Kendrick a handkerchief and she let the tears fall. When the phone rang, Kendrick lay down on the seat and cried harder. Her sister was going to hurt her, she just knew it.

"That was Danburn. I told him you'd talk to him later, that it was finished." Kendrick nodded at Noah. "I'm very sorry, my lady. I had no idea what sort of person she was until now. And I do believe I've never known someone who seemed to love saying the word 'castle' as much as she does."

"I saw that too. And I had no idea either, if you want to know the truth. I knew that she was needy and greedy, but never to this point. She actually thinks that no matter what I said to her, I'm going to continue to drop everything and run to her aid." He said that he could see that. "What will I do, Noah, when she calls me and tells me that she has no money and there is no food in the house?"

"You will do nothing, my lady. I will take care of her. And if there is something that I need from you, then I will ask. She will have to be cut off completely to understand that you mean what you say." She knew that too, but it didn't make it any less hard for her. "Danburn wanted to know if you would like to meet him in town for dinner tonight. I did explain to him that I thought you might need a night just snuggled on the sofa with him."

"And was he all right with that?" Because to Kendrick it sounded wonderful. "I'm sure he has a lot more things to do than to hold my hand because my sister hurt my heart."

"He said that he would bring you home a pretty. I have no idea what that might mean, but he is very happy to hold your hand, as well as the rest of you, because he knows that you're hurt." Kendrick nodded. "We have one more stop to make, my lady. Then we will head to the castle. All right?"

"Yes. But could you just call me Kendrick? You call Danburn by his given name. I'd very much like for you to do the same for me." He said it would be an honor. "You might not think so when my sister calls you fifty times a day."

"I'm made of good stock, Kendrick. And I've been around for some time. She cannot pull any wool over my eyes, and after today, I saw what sort of person she was. We'll get along just fine." Kendrick doubted that and hated to think he'd quit working for Danburn because of her sister. "Let me worry about her. You just enjoy being lady of the castle."

Yeah, lady of the castle. She wasn't sure she'd ever get used to being lady of anything. But she was going to try, damn it. As soon as she finished with the bank, signing all the required paperwork to get things rolling, she was going to fucking enjoy herself. She asked Noah how to do that, and he laughed all the way to the bank.

~~~

Danburn knew that she was resting on the couch. He'd been told by no less than ten people in the house that he was to let her rest, that she'd had a hard day. Noah had told him what had gone on with her sister and he'd tried to cut his day short to be with her. But things, like usual, got in the way, and he'd not been able to leave the office until an hour ago. Sitting on the chair across from her, he could see the tear stains on her cheeks and felt his heart twist up for it.

Danburn had sent someone to watch Louisa after he'd talked to Noah. And true to form, not only had Louisa gone out and spent nearly all of the money that she had, but she'd had a party too. The police had been called in twice to have them tone it down, and each time, the party had gotten more out of hand. It wasn't until the third time Jake and his men arrived that they ran the "guests" off and restored order to the neighborhood. Jake had also told Danburn what the apartment looked like when he was there. That conversation, and what he'd had to do after it, was what had made him late coming home.

"The furniture is gone. I don't mean destroyed, but simply gone. When I asked her about it, she told me that she had friends that were without. Since her sister was shacking up with you in the castle, she wasn't going to worry about it, because apparently she was going to be moving in with you two tomorrow anyway. I have a feeling that she's going to be a pain in your ass for a long time to come." Danburn told him she wasn't moving anywhere near them, but he only laughed at him. "The kitchen was full of booze as well as empties all over the yard. When I explained to her she'd need to clean that up, she waved me off like I was nothing more than a fly bothering her. That girl has some serious issues."

"You have no idea. She told Kendrick that I wasn't going to keep her. That in a few months, less really, I'd get tired of her and kick her to the curb. She seems to think that Kendrick is going to continue taking care of her until her death." Jake said that he got that as well. "But you did leave a man behind to keep track of her, right? At least until this thing with Bullock is gone."

"I did. I have men living across from her around the clock. And the cameras that we have set up at the doorways and windows are being watched all the time. You think this will bring him out? That Bullock will come for her?" He said that he thought so. "She sure is an easy target by the way things look. And the fact that she can't keep her mouth shut helps too."

"She's called Noah six times an hour since they left her. The only time she wasn't calling was when the party was in full swing, I guess." Danburn had made a drive by the house as he continued to talk to Jake on the phone. "Christ, she's at it again. There are two men moving out the bed while I'm sitting here watching."

"You want me to come by?"

He'd told him no, he would handle it. Then he'd made his way in to talk to her. He wished now that he'd let Jake handle it. Louisa was all over him the moment she saw him.

"I was wondering when someone was going to come by and help me move in with you two. You will have to have Kendrick give me her number. I can't be talking to that man all the time. He's not giving her any of my messages." Danburn had told her that he wouldn't either. "We're sisters. You can't keep us apart. Or is it that you want me...? Oh, I get it now. You and me, we're going to be getting it on while my sister is up there. You should have had someone tell me. The place is a mess now. I'll need a maid service—"

"I'm not sleeping with you." She asked him why not. "Because I'm going to marry your sister, and I don't particularly care for you."

"So? We can still have some fun. And if you pay me really nice I won't tell anyone either. I have to tell you, I did wonder why she was giving me this place to live in. And her telling me to get a job. Like that's going to happen. It's kind of silly to think that I'd need one once I'm living in the castle with you. Why would that matter? But now I understand...I have to be here for you, right?" He told her that he wouldn't be coming by. "Then you want me to come up to the castle. I understand we'll have to keep it quiet. I can do that."

"I'm not going to ever sleep with you, Louisa. Nor are you ever going to come to the castle to visit, much less live. You're here because you're Kendrick's sister, and that's all." She nodded and asked him how they were going to get it on, whatever that meant to her, if she wasn't to come to the castle right now. "I'm not sleeping with you."

"I'll need more things. As you can see, I've had to help out some of my friends. The bed — it wasn't really nice anyway — is going to a friend of mine who didn't have one, and then there is the couch and love seat. Another friend of mine didn't have any for his new place, and he loved the ones you put in here for me." Danburn had said nothing, but watched as two men struggled to get the bed into the back of a piece of shit truck. "You think I can get a bed tonight? With all your money, I bet that won't be any trouble. Or is this a good time for me to be coming up there to the castle? Kendrick said she had to get ready for me. It's all right if things aren't perfect yet."

"You gave away the only bed that I'm ever going to supply you with." She asked him where they were going to fuck. Just like that, where are we going to fuck. "I'm not going to touch you, not now, not ever."

"You mean because I don't have a bed. I bet you have a really nice one up at the castle we can use. Firm and everything." He'd turned to leave, but she grabbed his arm and it was all he could do to keep his beast under control. "I need some money too, if you have any. I'm going to talk to Kendrick soon about it, but since you're here and you're the one with the money, can you give me some until I speak to Kendrick?"

"No." He peeled her fingers off his arm and took a step away from her. "You've had your allotment for the month, Louisa. You'll have to either get a job or try to figure out what to do until then."

As he made his way to his car, she followed him. At first he thought for sure she was going to get in with him, just to make her way to his home, but she stood near the window and smiled at him. It wasn't the kind of smile he would have thought of coming from the shark she was, but one of sincerity. It occurred to him that she honestly believed that she was going to get her way. He drove home thinking about the way she'd made him feel so dirty.

"You look so serious." Danburn looked at Kendrick as she sat up on the couch, pulling him from his nightmarish thoughts. "Are you thinking of the old women and orphans you're tossing out this time of year?"

"No. I do that before lunch so that it doesn't interfere with my dinner plans." He watched her face and knew that she was still upset about today. "Come over here and sit on my lap. I want to tell you a story about when I was younger."

"I have a better idea. Why don't you come here, strip me out of my clothing, and make love to me?" His cock jerked in his pants. All day he'd thought of ways he wanted to take his new love, and that was when he realized that he had fallen in love with her. "I have on this new panty and bra set that I got today. And some other pretties that I want to tease you with."

"Show me." He smiled when she started to unbutton her blouse. Then she spread her legs wide enough that he could see a hint of yellow silk between her legs. "I love silk. Especially when it's on you."

The blouse was opened, but he could see little of the treats beneath it. When she sat up a little, using the back of the couch as leverage, she pulled the skirt she had on off and let it drop to the floor. Her legs opened for him, and he could see that she was wet, that she'd stained the silky material with her juices.

When she slid the blouse down her shoulders, she held it over her breasts. He wanted to see her, all of her, and reached down to stroke his cock through his pants. She moaned when he scooted down in his seat and opened his fly.

"I'd like to suck on your cock." He nodded, not sure he was able to speak around his sudden need to feel her doing just that. "Would you like that? To come down my throat?"

"Yes. Come here." She moved then, letting the blouse go, and he could see her dark nipples under the sheer material of her bra. "Take it off for me. Let me see all of you."

When she reached behind her to unhook her bra, Danburn pulled his pants down to his knees and wrapped his hand around his cock. He was painfully hard now. Pre-cum was dripping from the tip in a long stream, and he used it to fist himself. But when she took her bra off and dropped it to the floor with the rest of her clothing, he nearly jerked his dick off as she cupped her full breast and licked at the tip of it.

"Christ, do that again."

She did it to both her nipples, leaving them wet from her tongue. When she moved toward him, wearing only a pair of panties and her warm flesh, he wanted to beg her to let him eat her, but she was at his knees before he could make his tongue move to form words. When her hands moved to take his cock, he held onto the arms of the chair as she licked him from root to tip.

"You taste as good as you smell." Danburn nodded, not caring what she was saying so long as she finished him. When she took his crown in her mouth and sucked, he nearly came up out of the chair. "Don't touch me, Danburn. I want to explore you without you rushing me."

"I want to come in your mouth. On your body." Kendrick nodded at him and smiled. Then she leaned over him and

128

swallowed him down past the tightness of her throat.

He came. He might have thought that he could hold off, perhaps make it last longer, but as soon as she tightened those lovely muscles at the back of her throat around him, Danburn knew it was too much. Curling his hand at the back of her head, he filled her. His cock emptied deep into her and filled again as she fucked him with her mouth. Christ, he'd never been one to take his enjoyment before a woman, but he had a feeling that it was going to be hard for him not to with her. When he came a second time, his balls tight against his body, he pulled her up off the floor and jerked her down over his cock. The look on her face, the look of pure joy, had him taking them both to the floor and him plowing her hard.

"I want to come." He told her he wanted her to as well. "Please, fill me, Danburn. I want to feel you come inside of my pussy."

He held her body to his. Fucked her harder than he had any woman before her, and knew that she'd be sore in the morning. But the harder he took her, the more he fucked her, the more she begged him for. And when she dug her nails into his back and he felt the blood as it trickled down, Danburn felt her body tighten around his and she screamed out her release.

He watched her face as she came. Danburn knew that for as long as he lived the vision of her coming, her entire being releasing for him, would be something that he'd never forget. Something that would keep him warm on nights when she was sleeping beside him. As he threw back his head, his own body letting go, his dragon roared inside of him. Complete. He was, and they were, complete with this woman.

Dropping down on her, his body spent, he rolled to his back, holding her over him. His heart was aching it was pounding so hard. His breath was hot, his dragon letting him know that he was pleased as well. As he lay there, holding on to the woman who had come to mean more to him in the last week than any had in all his life, Danburn fell as deeply in love with his other half as he knew he was supposed to. Fletcher Danburn English, the ninth earl of the English castle, was in love with his mate.

# Chapter 9

"But you don't understand, Kendrick is supposed to take care of me. She has forever."

Noah rubbed at the pain that was beginning to take root between his eyes. For several days now he'd been dealing with Louisa Barrera at least a hundred times a day, and he was ready to throw in the towel. And when Kendrick came into the room with him, he had a feeling she knew he was at his wit's end with the other woman. She asked him for the phone.

"Louisa?" There was a pause, but even with the phone no longer in his hand, he could hear the other woman talking loudly to her sister. "Shut up and listen to me. You are not, under any circumstances, to call Mr. Noah again today. If you do, then I will no longer support you in that house you've nearly destroyed." Then she ended the call.

When Kendrick handed him back his phone, he sat down when she asked him to. He knew as surely as he was sitting there that things were not going to go well for the older woman. He decided to come clean with her.

"The apartment manager is ready to toss her out on her ear. The people who live across from her, hardened cops I'm to understand, have decided that if it comes to it, they'll gladly send her to Bullock if asked to. I doubt they really would, but you can understand where they are coming from." She said she did. "There is little furniture in the house, save the things that she wasn't able to give away, and the money that was to last her the month was gone, or nearly so, the first day."

"Have you given her any more?" He said that he had not. "Good. Don't. If you do, then she'll have won and you'll be broke in a week."

He wanted to assure her that he had plenty of money, but felt she might be right on this. Her sister was nothing like the young woman in front of him. When she got up to pace, he watched her with a new respect. She was his master's wife, or soon would be, the woman who ruled the household, and she wasn't afraid to admit that she didn't have any idea what she was doing.

"Three days ago I got a call from someone that you might know." He asked her who. "Julia James. She said that she and Danburn had been lovers, and that he made promises to her that she would like for me to take care of. She claims that he promised her two million dollars for her part of being his…his fuck buddy, she said."

"I don't think that—" Kendrick looked at him, and he leaned back on the couch. "They were lovers, I know this. For some years, but there was never any kind of agreement with her on that. She and her brother tried to scam Danburn just recently. He, Conrad Cortland, owned a housing development, and Danburn bought it from the bank. The loan. It's what he does."

"So this guy, Cortland, he tried to say what? That his sister was in love with Danburn and that he wanted money for her to go away, because of me?" Noah smiled. Kendrick's insecurity was showing through again. "I had nothing to do with that."

"No, my lady. Cortland wanted to continue on as the owner of the development, but for Danburn to foot the bill. He claimed that he had something that Danburn wanted in the form of Julia, because he'd kidnapped her. He wasn't aware that we knew they were related. But we knew differently." Kendrick sat down and asked him to tell her the story. "We were investigating the development, you see, because a friend of his had bought a home in the area. After several months of trying to get his home complete, to move into it safely, he called Danburn."

"You mean they were selling houses on spec?" He nodded, loving that he could have a conversation with her and not have to explain every detail. "So these houses, they were half-assed and not fit to be sold, and this man wanted to take Danburn to the cleaners so that...so that he could have his cake and eat it too sort of thing."

"Precisely. But there was a hang up. You see, Julia was starting to tell Danburn that she was broke. That her investments were not going as well as she had hoped. Her late husband had left her very well off, you see, so she should have been set for some time. Danburn had me look into what had happened." Kendrick smiled at him, and he knew she had figured it out. "I found that not only was her brother a part of the poor development planning, but the two of them had done this before. Bought land, put up a very lovely spec home as you called it, and then started the other homes with no intentions of finishing them. No cabinet tops, bathrooms with no shower or toilet. Some of the rooms would have no carpet, but others would only have half a room. It was terrible."

"Okay, so this guy, he does his little scam thing and has his sister try to get more from Danburn to help them start their next little game. I'm missing something, aren't I?" He nodded and laughed when she told him to give her a moment to see if she could figure it out. Noah watched as her mind seemed to work it out. "Okay, so this guy has this scam. But his sister is working her own, namely against Danburn. Then he unknowingly buys the note from the bank and the scammers figure out they can really get his ass and his money. So they… the Feds would be involved, because basically if they borrowed money from the bank in a fraudulent way, then they would be on the hook for that. And blackmail too. I'm assuming that is what they were trying again, blackmailing Danburn in the way of…you said he wanted to continue on as before, so this guy wanted to sell the houses after Danburn fixed them for him, and he used Julia in that plot somehow."

"He claimed that he had kidnapped her and that she would be returned to Danburn once the contract between them was signed." Noah hadn't had this much fun in ages. "But his lordship was already aware that they were related, as I said, and had had them followed. When it came time for us to go to the meeting with Cortland, his sister was arrested at the airport, tickets in hand, ready to flee the country."

Kendrick smiled at him. "So she's in jail and not at her lovely apartment that she claims Danburn set up for her. One that he visits every day when he's told me he was at work." Noah told her that he was not with her. "How the hell is she getting out to call me then? I mean, don't they have rules for that kind of shit?"

"I'm sure there are, but I will have Jake look into it. She might have privileges that we are unaware of." Noah pulled out his note pad and wrote to check on that. When Kendrick sat down across from him, he thought there might be more that she needed from him. "My lady?"

"I have this thing with Danburn tomorrow night." He nodded. "It's formal and all. I can do that part, the dress up thing, but I have no idea what I'm supposed to be doing. I mean…do I just hang on his arm and smile at people? Am I going to be required to have a conversation with them? I can talk about my sister, my job situation, and how to not walk in heels. After that, I'm pretty much used up."

"You should be yourself. I do believe that is what made Danburn fall in love with you." She snorted and he frowned. "You do not believe that he loves you?"

"He doesn't. But this party thing. Will there be a dinner? I mean, will I have to know which fork to use for what sort of food?" Noah was wondering why she didn't believe that Danburn loved her when something occurred to him. She had no idea that she loved him too. "Noah?"

"There will be only petite plate food. Things on a long buffet table that you will pick for yourself. Drinks too. Champagne, I believe, as well as other items. I'm aware that you do not drink, so I would ask them for water with a lime or lemon in it. You will appear to be a snob that way." She asked him if she was supposed to be a snob. "Yes. They are a group that are as stale and mean as you are fresh and honest. I would wish that you could have more time, get to know some of these people better before you are subjected to them, but I do believe that you will be able to hold your own. Be yourself, my lady, and you will shine."

"I don't know about all that. What is this thing for,

135

anyway? He just said he's the guest of honor. How?" Noah told her that Danburn was quite the humanitarian. "I see. So he is generous with his millions and they're going to spend it to have a party for him."

"I do believe that one of the charities he has donated to is throwing this thing. So yes, I guess you would be correct." He'd never really thought of it that way before. "But I do believe that they're going to be charging others for this opportunity to attend."

"You know that's nuts, right? Give a party for some man who has given you money to do whatever it is you need. Then when he gets there, hit him up for more. Why not have an open dinner with everyone who can afford to paying up, and that way no one is out? Then maybe have an auction of donated items to defray the costs of the shindig." He smiled at her and she grinned back. "As you can tell, I'm not big on charities. I'm sure that most of them do what they say they're going to do, but there are a lot of them that only profit for the big wigs. I know one that has everything donated to them, so it's one hundred percent profit. Then they sell the items off and pay their workers very little because they end up with a tax break for hiring people who have special needs. I think their CEO makes like two million a year, and none of the money he says is for charities actually goes to anyone."

"I have heard of this too." The more time he spent with Kendrick the more he liked her. His first opinion of the young woman was so far off the mark that he was ashamed that he'd thought it. "This charity, the one honoring Danburn, is one of those sort of charities. And I do believe that after this, he won't be giving any more money to them. He's done his homework too."

"My sister isn't going to go away, is she?" The change in

subject startled him into not having a ready answer for her. But she didn't seem to require one as she answered her own question. "She won't. She will continue to try and take and take from anyone that will answer her until they are as broken as she is. And that won't stop her either. She'll just keep at you until you have to run and hide from her to get away. Or die."

"You won't die." He knew she was aware of this, but he wanted her to remember that it would not last forever, this thing with her sister. "I have made sure — on several occasions — that she is not getting anything more from you or Danburn. But she is most…I was going to say persistent, but that's not it either, is it? She just hears what she wants, and the rest is just mumbling to her."

"Right after I was released from the hospital and living with a foster parent, she came to me in the middle of the night. Just came into the house like it was hers and got into bed with me. I was so afraid of her that I wasn't sure what to do but lie there. I thought for sure she'd come to finish the job. Then the next morning she came down to breakfast with me like she was supposed to be there. The foster family had to call the police to get rid of her. Several days later I saw her again, this time with Mom. They were both so disappointed in me for not making sure that they had a place to live as nicely as I did." Noah knew this. He'd done a very thorough background check on the entire family before he knew her. "My mom went on and on about how it wasn't her fault that I'd been shot, that she'd needed a place to stay, and since I was the youngest that she'd not loved me like she had Louisa. It was then that I knew there was never going to be any kind of relationship between the two of us."

"She died a few years ago, did she not?" Kendrick told him that she'd been on the run until then, wanted for attempted murder. "Yes. And your sister, she'd been staying with her off and on. I believe that she even spent some time in jail as well."

"Yes. For a great many things. But they'd let her out when, in my opinion, they could no longer stand her. Then she'd hit me up for money, and when that didn't work because I'd not have it, she'd come to my place, steal what she could, and blame me for it." Noah's heart broke for Kendrick. She'd had such a hard and unloved childhood. "When she calls again, let me know. I'm going to end this once and for all."

He wasn't sure he should do that. Louisa was dangerous. Not in a way that she would mean to harm someone, but she would sell out Kendrick somehow to get whatever she wanted. But he agreed he'd do it. However, Danburn would know as well.

~~~

Bernie knew where the woman was. Knew everything there was to know about her, including the fact that the police and the Feds were watching her. He wasn't sure it was because of him. The woman had some enemies of her own, but he had a feeling that some of her being under the watchful eye of some pretty powerful Federal agents was due to him. He wasn't sure what to do about it either.

"Two days ago she had a visitor from the English household. Not sure what was said—can't get in there with some devices they have about—but when he left, she was pretty angry. Broke a few windows out and threw rocks at him." The more that Bernie heard about this girl from Collier, the more he liked her. She was going to die, but he did admire her spunk. "Her bills as well as her rent are paid by English. There's a cell phone in the household, but I can't get to it to clone it to see who she's calling. The men across from her are watching but don't seem to interact with her. And I don't think she has any idea what they're doing there."

"You think he's her lover, this English person?" Collier said he didn't believe so. The one time he'd been there, which had been days ago, he didn't strike him as even liking the woman. "So what is he doing taking care of her? I know that the sister is in on this somehow, but who the hell has any knowledge of her either? Do you think he's keeping her nice and happy so he can fuck the sister? I've heard she's a beauty. Could be that's it."

"I have no idea. I'm telling you, Bernie, it's like there is this shield around the castle and no one can get on that property without ten men coming after them. Twice now I've sent men there, and they got no further than the trees before they were caught and escorted off the place. It's almost as if the land is talking to them." Bernie said nothing. It had been like that too when he'd been walking along the land, seeing if he could get a closer look at the castle he wanted. "And that office that English works in is like a fucking fortress. You can't get in the door without a badge. There is so much security in that place that getting a man even to sneak in the kitchen is impossible. It's as if he has national secrets in there."

"He has to have a staff. Someone needs to leave the place to get supplies or some shit." Collier said that he did, they lived there. "What the fuck is he doing there? Running a fucking city on his property? I'm telling you right now, when I get that place, and I will, things will be different."

He'd never even seen the inside of the place, but knew that it would need updates. He had a feeling that it would have cold stone walls and floors in need of some thick warm carpet. English was old school and would have, in his opinion, left things the way they were in order to preserve the magic of the place. Or some shit like that. He also thought the place would be filled with old furniture. Well cared for, but still it would be older than his great grandmother. Bernie wanted new. Everything new and modern.

"Also, you're not going to like this either, but there is no one on that police force that is going to play ball with you. And trust me, I looked hard. There isn't a dishonest person on the payroll, not to mention there is nothing I can find on the mayor or anyone else that might have some influence to getting someone in your pocket." Bernie said that wasn't possible. "Not only is it possible, but I think anyone in this town would lay down and die for English should he ask them to."

"What the hell does this guy do? Blow them every time he comes into town? Nobody is that nice, nor are they that clean. Dig deeper. There has to be something." He looked at Collier when he didn't move to do what he'd told him. "You have something else to add to this shit?"

"There is a rumor, a big one but just a rumor, that English is a dragon." Bernie waited for the punch line, but when one was not forthcoming, he asked him if the person was on drugs. "Not that I'm aware of. But there have been some sightings here and there. And that man and his family have been around forever, I guess. Well before the town grew up around the castle. I've looked, and they're right. The castle has been in the same hands since it was built. And this English is the ninth earl to have lived there."

"You're kidding me, right? You really expect me to believe that there is a dragon that lives around here and it's not only a rumor? That no one, not even me, who has been here for nearly four months, have heard shit about it, nor have I seen it? And I'm pretty sure that I would have remembered seeing a dragon flying around." Collier told him again it was just a rumor. "Don't bring me shit like that again. I don't have time for it."

After Collier left, saying he had some errands to run, Bernie sat at his desk and tried to think what the hell he was going to do to end this shit. There was no one to keep him abreast of the cops in town. He had a neighbor that was less than friendly, and who had made no bones about wanting Bernie and his operations to be gone from here. He had a witness to a murder that he'd committed, and no one had come out to arrest him, yet. And a nosey cop that could show up at any time to have a "tour" of the work he did.

The deal that was going down tonight would net him millions of dollars. The cove just beyond his property — on English's property, actually — was ideal for shipments going out and coming in. Bernie doubted that anyone had used the place in decades, yet it had been set up with the kind of dark secrecy that he needed.

In addition to the inlet that was under the property, an existing dock was available that had only needed some minor repairs, along with electricity that lit the cove up like a fucking mall on Christmas Eve. He'd already sent out one shipment this way, and had received a dozen or so others. Bernie thought that this place had been made with him in mind.

Standing up, he was making his way to the door when he remembered that Angel was gone. Thank goodness for that. He was going to have to explain to her mom that she'd not worked out, and how she'd taken off with some man. She'd believe it. The apple in that family didn't fall far from the tree.

Getting in his cart, he made his way to the cove. He wanted it to be ready for tonight, and for nothing to go wrong with this shipment. The last time had been a sort of test run. Tonight was going to be big, and the man on the other end, the man receiving the shipment, promised more orders if this went well. Bernie wanted it to go very well. But as soon as he made it to the mouth of the cove, he knew something was wrong.

The dock was completely destroyed, and not only was there nothing left but splinters of wood, it had been cleaned up and neatly stacked along the walls of the cave like they were going to come back for it. The wiring that had hung down in long black snake-like strands had also been torn down, and it too was wrapped in a neat coil right next to the wood. Someone had not just come in and taken out his way of life, but they had made sure that he knew it wasn't an accident. Standing there, his entire business fucked right now, he sat down to answer his phone when it went off.

"You there yet? I can tell that you're standing on the rocks. But it's not easy to pinpoint just where you are at the moment." He asked the person what they were talking about. "The cove. You've seen it, haven't you? The way that I've taken the liberty of cleaning up after you? I mean, when you take someone else's land and use it for wrong, you have to expect some sort of consequences, don't you?"

"Who the hell is this? English? I want to know, because as soon as I find you, I'm going to murder you. You fucking asshole. What the hell were you thinking?" The man, he knew it was a man now, was laughing at him. "Do you know what this is going to cost me?"

"I do, as a matter of fact. An entire shipment of drugs you're making on that property not going out on time. A shame, that. Your buyer is not going to be happy with you about it. And when someone asks you about line running, you should probably know there is no such thing. He wanted to trip you up, and it worked like a charm." Bernie looked around, wondering how the hell the man knew what he'd been doing down here. "I have no use for cameras, Bernie. I have other means of keeping an eye on you. And the well that you dropped those three men in, I'm going to make sure that someone finds that soon too. Oh, and you might want to ask Collier what he did with your niece. I'm pretty sure she's going to turn up sooner than you think. The story he told you is a lie. He snapped her neck the moment you left him to take care of her."

"What are you talking about? My niece ran off with some man." The laughter again. It was sending shivers down his spine, it was so cold and harsh. "Who is this?"

"Your niece didn't run off with anyone, now did she? It's not very sporting of you to lie to me when I know the truth. Ask Collier what he did with her body. I'm sure that once you hear his side of the story, you're going to wish you hadn't. It's a terrible one, to say the least. And I have decided that I will tell you who this is. Your neighbor, though I'm pretty sure you've guessed that by now." Bernie stood up and moved out of the cave. He'd known that it belonged to English, but how did he find out that Bernie had used it? "If I were you, Bernie, I'd pack up my little operation and leave town before I have to make you. And when I say I'll make you, I want you to know that no one, not even men with the best kind of equipment, will ever find your body when I'm done with you."

The line went dead, but Bernie was no less terrified of the sounds that came from his phone. Several things were running through his mind. First of which, how had English gotten his phone number? The next few items were, what did he mean about his niece, who was going to find her body, and how had he found out about the pit of dead workers?

# Chapter 10

Danburn looked at Noah when he laughed. The two of them had been plotting all day, and now that it was finished, he felt sort of let down. The phone call to Bernie had worked well, and now that he'd done it, he needed to do more. But something was tickling Noah and he wanted to be a part of it. Asking him had given him nothing, the man was laughing that hard.

"I'm having so much fun now." Danburn smiled. It was infectious, his laughter. "First the lady of the house, and now this. When you were telling me about how you'd taken care of the inlet, I had all sorts of visions in mind, but to have had your dragon go there and simply step on things was wonderful. What would he have done, you suppose, should he have caught him there?"

"I'm sure that this might have ended then, and not been stretched out like it is now. And besides, I'm pretty sure that now that he's pissed, he's going to make some major mistakes that we can capitalize on." Noah nodded. "Have you any word from Louisa?"

"Daily. And it's the same thing over and over. When are we coming to get her? The money that Kendrick promised is not here. There is no bed. When can she expect that to be taken care of? Then the castle again. I think, as I was saying to Kendrick, that Louisa likes to say that word. Castle, castle, castle."

"Kendrick wants to see him, my beast." That shut Noah up, and he looked at him with his mouth opened. "I have tried to tell her that he is not like the dragons that are in story books, or those that are in those romance novels. But she insists and I cannot turn her down."

"Kendrick will be terrified of you." Danburn nodded. He knew what he looked like as his beast. It was why he called him that. He was large, scaled, and had claws that could tear into stone without problems. "You cannot let her see you, sir. If you do, she would be scarred for life."

"I have an idea that she would be frightened, but I think you might be exaggerating it a little." Noah said that he didn't think so. "Well, it's a moot point now. She has asked and I've told her yes. We're going down to the lake this evening, and I will show her there."

"The lake? Where you swim? What if she tells someone that is what you do?" Danburn started to tell him she'd never do that, but he answered his own statement. "Nay, she would never turn you in. She is in love with you. And you her."

"She said she doesn't love me." Noah didn't bother telling Danburn that he knew he was in love with Kendrick. He'd been telling him that for days. But Noah just waved him off. "I have asked her, Noah. She said that she likes me well enough, but she doesn't love me."

"Because she's had no idea what it is to love someone. Or to be loved." Danburn watched as his friend got up to walk around the room. "She has an appointment with her sister tomorrow. I have asked to go with her, but she said that she has to do this on her own. I don't know that I'd want to be in Louisa's shoes at this moment. I do think that my lady plans to tear her a new butt. But she said she'd be home in plenty of time to get dressed and ready for the event. I think she's more nervous about that than you are."

Danburn had no doubt that Kendrick had it in her, but he still didn't want her alone right now. Threatening Bernie over the phone was one thing, but he might take matters into his own hands and hurt those that he loved. His mother could take care of herself, he knew this, but Kendrick was only human. Even as his mate, she would still be hurt.

Danburn was ready to order Noah to be with Kendrick when his door opened, and there stood Kendrick with his mom. They'd been in town earlier today, getting last minute things for the honorary dinner, and were to meet him for lunch with Noah. He stood up as his mom started telling him that it was all right. It had been handled.

"Kendrick? What is it, love?" Instead of answering him, she sat down on the chair across from his desk and stared. He was worried and looked at his mom, who looked concerned too. "What's happened?"

"Her sister was in town today, and they had a...I would call it a meeting of the minds. It really is too bad that you missed it. It was quite entertaining to say the least." He asked her what had happened. "I believe that Louisa is well aware of her sister being finished with her. She might not heed it, but she does know that Kendrick is done with her."

"She tried to steal my purse. And Elissa's." They all turned to look at Kendrick when she finally spoke. "I guess stealing isn't really how she saw it. She said that she wanted my wallet and the cards in it, and took it. I have no idea why she thought that I'd just turn it over to her, but she really was upset with me when I called security on her."

"Did she hurt you?" Kendrick looked at him and smiled. It was sad to say the least, but she did look like she was with him and not back at whatever had happened today. "What did you say to her?"

"I told her we were done. And that when she gets out of jail, if she does, then the locks would be changed on the apartment and that the money was gone. I'm well aware of the fact that she spent this month's money in one day, but she won't be getting any more. I...I hope you don't mind, but I went ahead and changed the locks, and told the bank to stop payment on the account."

"Yes. Whatever you need to do." Danburn glanced at his mom when she laughed. "Thank you for helping her."

"I didn't do anything. She did this all on her own. The only thing she asked me for was the name of the bank. The rest of it she did like she knew just what had to be done. It was a sight to see, her getting all bossy like. I loved every minute of it."

Kendrick asked him if he thought she was incapable of taking care of things.

"No. I just wondered who I was going to have to kiss for helping you. Where is she now?" Kendrick told him she'd been taken to jail. "Good. Why don't you tell me what happened? That way I can act like your knight in shining armor when someone asks me about it."

"You goof." He smiled when she did. "Your mom and I were looking at a dress that had only just arrived at the shop.

148

I fell in love with it, and we were just talking about me trying it on. As I took it to the dressing room, the door opened and there was Louisa. She told me that she wanted me to give her money. That she…that as her sister, I didn't want to see her without."

"I had wandered away to find shoes for the dress when she entered the dressing room, or she would never have gotten that far." Danburn nodded at his mom when she picked up the story. "But when I returned, I could hear them talking. Well, Kendrick was talking, Louisa was shouting."

"She told me how I'd tricked her into keeping away from me. That I was treating her badly by not talking to her when she wanted to ask me something. I asked her what she wanted that didn't have to do with me forking over something that I had. You should have seen the look on her face. It was like she had no idea what I was talking about." Danburn would just bet that Louisa hated that Kendrick was telling her no more and more. "I told her that she had signed a contract with you and me, and that if she didn't uphold her part of the bargain, like getting a job and making a living for herself, she'd be out on her ass. Then she slapped me."

"She hit you?" Danburn might have laughed at the indignant sound of Noah's voice, but the man continued before he could tell him that he'd take care of Louisa himself. "Why, the nerve of that woman, hitting you like you were nothing. I should like to find her and tell her a thing or two about royalty and how they are to be treated."

"I hit her back, Noah. But I thank you." Kendrick looked at Danburn and winked as she told him the rest. "She kept going on and on about how we were sisters and that I should want her to have nicer things than me. That I should be living in the apartment and her living in the castle with you. And I'm pretty sure she thought she should be in your bed too. Then she told me that Mom said to her that I was undeserving of the life I had after I'd been injured. That I should have given them more when I had it so good. Injured? Like she didn't try to kill me? And when I asked Louisa about that, she said that it wasn't Mom's fault that I was shot, it was mine for being a selfish person and ungrateful to them. For not being happy that it was me and not Louisa that had been shot."

"She believes that you should have taken the bullet willingly because she's your sister, and that's what sisters want for each other?" Kendrick told him that was nearly what she'd said, word for word. "Mother fuck, she's a fruit ball."

"Danburn." He looked up at his mom and asked her what she'd call her. "I mean the *mother fuck* part, not the fruit ball part. But I must agree, she is off her noodle a bit. Has she had any kind of testing done, Kendrick?"

"Yes. A few years ago she was tested to figure out if she could be accountable for her own actions. I had refused to pay for a car that she totaled because she wanted to see what it was like to drive really fast. I explained to the judge what I'd been going through for the past ten years, and he had her evaluated." Danburn asked her what they'd figured out. "That while she's very selfish and materialistic, there is nothing wrong with her mentally. She has a very high IQ that she doesn't use until she wants to manipulate someone, and she can do that hands down."

"I'll say." Danburn looked at Noah when he spoke. "I have heard from the men who are watching her that she has no less than five times gotten free pizzas delivered to her, and convinced the mailman to slip her things under the door rather than make her go down to the mailbox on the first floor to get it."

"That sounds like her." Danburn sat down in front of Kendrick and took her hands into his. They were cold but as he held them, the warmer they got. "She told me that I had to help her, and that she still hadn't heard when we were going to come and get her to move into the castle. Then she reached over and took my purse and started going through it like I had not just told her no. She had the nerve to tell me she was disappointed in me, that I only had two hundred dollars on me, and stuck it in her pocket before taking Elissa's bag too."

"I was so shocked that I could only stand there and stare at her as she dumped the contents of my bag on the floor. The nerve of her. And when she figured out that I had no cash on me whatsoever, she told me I'd have to start carrying some from now on, it was my duty as Kendrick's friend." His mom laughed. "I'm pretty sure that the officer that arrested her is getting an earful about now."

"Why is that?" Kendrick laughed when his mom did. "Oh, this is going to be good. What did you do to her?"

"We didn't do anything to her or him. Tempting, but no, nothing. But Louisa did tell the officer that he was to call you so that you could come and get her. Fetch her, is what I believe she said. That as you are the lover to her sister, it was the only right thing he could do." His mom laughed again as she finished. "Then she went on to tell him to explain to you that you were to bring her more money, that she wanted pretty things like her sister. That she also wanted to be staying at the castle with you, because the apartment that she had wasn't fit for her any longer."

Danburn wasn't sure what he could do with this woman to get her out of their life. She was a nuisance, yes, but she was also Kendrick's sister. He figured that he'd go and talk to her, one more time. She had to understand what she was doing to her sister. Or maybe not. Either way, he wasn't going to leave until she had it firmly in her head that there was nothing more coming from either of them.

~~~

Louisa had wanted to go out and find her sister, but the officer that had put her in here told her that she wasn't going to be able to leave until he said so. And even telling him that her sister was going to be upset with him didn't stop him from ignoring her. Louisa knew that as soon as Kendrick found out where she was, she was going to be right here to get her out.

And they had taken her money…all of it, and more than likely would not be giving it back to her. Kendrick wasn't going to be happy about that either. As soon as Louisa got to live in the castle, things were going to be looking up for her.

That was completely unnecessary of him to do that, she thought. It was hers after all. Kendrick had given it to her. Well, not given it to her, but she had made sure that she had it. And that other woman with her, what was her deal? Why had she been so upset when Louisa had wanted her to carry money as well? What did they think was going to happen to her if she didn't have money? There were things that only worked with money.

As for the apartment, Louisa wasn't worried about that either. As soon as Kendrick came down here and got her out of this mess, she was going to the castle with her. It was just stupid for them to be paying for that place and the castle, when they could just give her the rent money they were paying plus the money that had been promised her, and she'd be happy. And with all the things in the castle that she knew were going to be expensive and lovely, Louisa knew that she'd be living in style.

Kendrick was just being mean to make her see some point.

152

Her sister was forever trying to make her see things her way. Louisa had news for her, no one saw things the way Kendrick did. She was going to have to just give up on that. Louisa liked things just the way she wanted them, and it was Kendrick's responsibility to make sure that she had them.

When she heard someone coming down the hall, she stood up. Louisa wanted them to bring her a nicer bed and a blanket that wasn't itchy. There had to be something nicer for her somewhere. She was going to live in a castle and they should want her to have prettier things. And if they didn't have it here, they would have to call Kendrick and have her get it for her. But when that man, Danburn, stood in front of the room she was in, Louisa backed away from him.

"You're being a pain in the ass. As I'm sure you're aware of." She asked him what he was talking about, she'd done nothing to anyone. "What about today, when you accosted Kendrick and my mom? I suppose you think you were justified in that too?"

"Your mom? She can't be your mom. She didn't even have a dollar on her to give to me when Kendrick gave me what she had. And I know she had credit cards there that she could have gotten an advance on. But she refused me. What did Kendrick say about that? I bet she was really mad." He sat down in the chair that was brought in for him. She wanted service like that, and told the cop that had brought it for him to get her silk sheets and a nice pretty pillow. He just kept walking. "I don't think they know what I am to you, do they?"

"And what is it you think you are to me? Other than a pain in the ass, like I said." She wasn't sure what he was asking her, and told him to explain himself. "I'm nothing to you right now. In a few days, when Kendrick and I get married, I suppose you'll be my sister-in-law, but right now you're nothing."

"I'm something. I think I'm very special." He only stared at her. "Where is Kendrick? I want you to tell her that she needs to come and see me. And to bring me the money that she owes me. Those men, they took what she already gave me. And you might want to tell her that she needs to hurry up with getting my rooms ready up there. I'm sick of not having things of my own."

"How does she owe you money? And I know for a fact that you've been told several hundred times that you're not living in our home." Louisa wasn't sure how to answer that and told him again to get her sister. "She doesn't owe you anything, Louisa. Surely you can see that."

"She's my sister, and I know that she wants the best for me. I need money and she has it. Why are you making this difficult? I want you to get her for me now, and for you to go away. I don't like you. And so you know, I wouldn't plan on getting married to her. You can't marry her because I don't want her to marry. She'll do what I want because she's my sister." He only looked at her like he was confused. "Kendrick wants what's best for me. She always has. I love the fact that she provides me with a good life. I need her to keep doing that. Even after we're living in the castle, I think we'll not be having anything to do with you."

"So you don't want her to marry so you can continue to manipulate her into giving you whatever you want." There was a trick there. She knew it, but he was too slick for her to figure it out right now. Louisa told him again to get Kendrick. "I'm not going to get her for you. She's had enough stress from you to last several lifetimes."

"She's stressed because she worries about me all the time. She won't have to worry so much when I move into the castle with her. I won't have to try and find her all the time either, when I want something." He said nothing again, and she thought she might hate this man. "You're not nice at all. You know that, right? And when Kendrick gets here, I'm going to tell her you won't do as I say."

"No, I won't. And Kendrick isn't coming here. She asked me to take care of you." Well that sounded better. She asked him how much he had on him for now. "I'm not going to give you money, Louisa. That's not how she asked me to take care of you."

"Then what? What are you going to give me? I know, you're to take care of my living arrangements, but I can't be there forever. The castle, that's where I need to be. With my sister. I want a room of my own at the castle, and servants. I know that there are some there, but I want my own. Someone that can run a bath for me and help me pick out my clothes for the day." She smiled at him. "This might be better than money anyway. I can sell whatever is in my room that I don't want, right? I mean, you and Kendrick want me to have a lovely room, just the way I want it, right?"

"You're not living in the castle." She nodded, knowing that he'd give in sooner or later. Everyone always did for her. "You really do believe that you should have whatever you want whenever you think you need it, don't you?"

"And why not?" She sat down on the bed that she hated and wondered why he found this so hard to believe. "I have needs like everyone else does. I want things, sometimes more than others, but I want them. Kendrick has a job, or she did, but now she has money anyway. Money that she gets from you. Why shouldn't she provide for me, like she's always done? As my sister, she wants to do those things she does for me. You should too. I'm not a mean person. I just know what I want, and you should want to get them for me."

"No." Louisa was used to hearing that word from people. They'd say it to her all the time, right up until she drove them to say yes. It was what she'd done all her life, and she didn't see why Danburn thought he should be immune to her. When he stood up, she thought that he was finally getting it.

"I think this will work out pretty good, don't you? And when are you sending me a car? I want to arrive in style. Can you take my picture as I get out of it? I want a big limo with a driver in a suit." He said nothing as he folded the chair back up and put it under his arm. "Tell Kendrick that I want a room with a pretty view. Oh, never mind. I'll pick out the room I want when I get there. I think there should be a party too. You know, in honor of me living there with you. I can give you a list if you have some paper and a pen."

He didn't pull out any paper, and he didn't seem to have a pen with him. As he moved down the hall, Louisa shouted at him that she'd be here when he got back, to not wait too long. About an hour later, she was still thinking of things to have at her homecoming party when another man came to stand in front of her little room.

"Did Danburn send you here to make the list? I've been thinking that it might be better if we have it the day after tomorrow instead of when I get home. I'll need some new clothes to wear before then." He just stood there, and she stood up see if she needed to take something from him. "Did Kendrick send you? You have money for me from her?"

"No. I have nothing from your sister or English." She didn't know who that was and asked him about it. "Danburn English. And you're going to get me into his house."

"Oh yes, I can do that. They're throwing a party for me, you see. And I'm going to make sure that they invite the entire town to it. And gifts too. Everyone will want to bring me a gift, being that I'm related to Kendrick and all." He pulled out a key and unlocked the door on her room. "Thank you very much."

Just as she moved by him, ready to tell him all about the party they were having, he jerked her to him and put a cloth over her mouth. She felt her body swaying even as the man told her she was going to be very helpful indeed.

There were sounds that hurt her ears as the man carried her out of the cell. She knew that she was on his shoulder, because she could see his butt and the floor was moving. But no matter how hard she tried, she couldn't get her mouth to work to tell him to put her down. And that her belly was sick.

Loud popping noises seemed to wake her from a dream. Noises that reminded her of the time in the lake, when those men tried to kill her for no reason. A memory of that time tickled at her head, but she was sick now and felt like she was in one of those carnival rides that swung you around over and over.

When she opened her eyes the next time, she knew that she'd been put in a box or something. And the way she was being tossed around made her think that perhaps she'd been put in a van for reasons she could not even begin to know. She wanted a limo, not a van. Trying to lift her hands to take the cover off her mouth, she realized that she was tied up.

Kidnapped. She'd been kidnapped. Louisa was giddy at the prospect of being kidnapped, and could not wait to see Kendrick's face when she paid the ransom and got her home. This was going to make them give her everything she wanted, that was for sure.

# *Chapter 11*

Danburn lifted his head from the water. No more than a few inches, enough that he could see her sitting on the bank and watch her. He was afraid of scaring her, and more afraid of making her hate him. But she only stared at him as he moved closer to the edge of the water to see her.

"You're very large, aren't you?" He nodded, just making it so that his head moved and the water stayed still. "Are you going to come out of the water, or do I have to guess at what you're hiding from me?"

*I'd rather just stay here.* She nodded but only sat there. *Yes, I'm very large, much too big to want to come out of the water until you're ready for me.*

"So this wasn't going to be me seeing you. It was going to be you hiding in the water like some wimpy dick." He lifted his head out of the water a little more, just so she could see his nose but not his mouth. "Do you have monster teeth?"

*Yes.* He slowly brought his head out of the water, careful

to keep an eye on her as he did. *Aren't you worried that I might come at you? Hurt you?*

"No. I worry about a lot of things, but not you hurting me. Come out of the water to your shoulders. I'm assuming that you have them." He said that he did, but he wasn't pretty. "You are to me. Handsome, I guess you'd be."

*I'm a beast, not one of the pretty dragons that you see in movies.* She leaned back on her hands, and he lifted his head. *I have hands that would kill you with just a touch.*

"But you won't hurt me. Come out, Danburn. I want to see all of him." He should have thought this through better, he realized. Showing her his dragon would give her bad dreams. He knew there were some things that no one could be prepared for. "If you don't come out of the water for me, I'm going to go home and leave you here all alone. And I had such plans for us on the grass."

*Like what?* She lifted her blouse up and over her head, and lifted her bare breasts up to her mouth. When her tongue touched a hard tip, he growled low. *You are not playing fair.*

"Come out of the water." He moved then, slowly so as not to overwhelm her. But he should have known better. There was nothing about this woman that was like other people. As he stretched out, his wings spreading to dissipate the water from them, she lay back on the grass and he lifted his body from the water completely.

It had been a very long time since he'd been free like he was now. She looked very tiny there below him, and he was extra careful where he stepped. She said nothing when he put his claw down to touch it to her skin, and when he nicked her, causing the smallest of wounds, all she did was watch him as he lowered his head to lick the wound closed. His tongue was bigger than her, his teeth, long and sharp, would have impaled her from head to toe with more left hanging. Danburn had never had his size be so obvious to him before.

*He has your taste now, his own taste of you.* She asked him what that meant. *That he can find you should you be lost to us. You're his too. You know that, don't you?*

"You talk as if he were another being. Is he?" He wasn't sure what she meant and asked her. "Do you think of yourself as a whole, or are you two different people?"

*There are times when he takes me. Anger or fear will cause him to consume what I am. I believe that he does this so that I cannot know what sort of monstrous things he does when it's needed.* He sat, leaned down beside her, and put out his hand. *Should you like to have a ride, my love? Not in the sky…we can do that later when the darkness can hide me. But now, as I walk around the forest.*

She readily climbed into his outstretched hand and they moved into the trees, taking the path that he had worn down over the decades. She had put her blouse back on. He was slightly disappointed, but less distracted by her nudity. When she laughed, he felt his dragon grin at him. This was what it must have been like when dragons roamed the earth.

"How do you hide from the humans of the world?" He let his body merge into the trees, the color of his scales matching perfectly with the trees around him. His legs were brown in some places, green and dark like the earth in others to fade into the grounds as he stood beside them. "That's fantastic. To be so hidden in plain sight like this."

*It has its handiness. Several times over the years I've had to use this method. When a family came to picnic by the lake, unknowingly on my property, I had to stand still for over three hours. I was only glad that I had gone to the bathroom just prior to me noticing them.* He laughed when she did. *I should like to swim with you now. If you've a mind to.*

"The water will be so cold, won't it?" He told her that it was as warm as a bath year round. "The earth does that for you?"

*Nay, I for her. She can replenish her waters and fish for me. When the dragon is here, he will feast as much as he can.* She asked him if he enjoyed being his dragon. *Never have I as much as I have today.*

Moving into the lake with her in his hand, he held her up as he lay back. When she stood upon his belly, walking the length of him, Danburn thought that this was the greatest thing that had ever happened to him. To have a mate that cared not what he looked like as his beast.

*She is yet unaware of the dangers that lurk around us.* The voice of his dragon startled Danburn. It had been so long since he'd had to speak to him that he paused before asking him what he meant. *The men from the woods, they are seeking vengeance against you. Should she be hurt, there will be no stopping my fury.*

*Any person, human or not, that touches her will die.* His dragon agreed. *We'll have to make sure that she's safe while they're about. Can you feel them, when they move upon the earth?*

*I can. You can as well, but not as well as me. The man who you spoke to on the speaking device, he is light in step. I feel he is glad for something. I will speak to the lady of the grounds, see what she has to share. But not yet. Yonder comes your man, Noah. He is not light, his steps are fast and hard. I feel he is bringing bad news to our happy time.*

Just as Noah appeared in the tree line, he pulled Kendrick to him. He had no idea if Noah was being chased or not, but he was going to protect her with his life.

"I should like to speak to you, my lord. Now." Danburn sat Kendrick on the shoreline and moved beneath the water to shift. It wasn't necessary to do so, but it was painful for him sometimes, and he didn't want her to be fearful of this after having such a glorious day. Dragon spoke again.

*He has kidnapped a young woman. She is in trouble even as we speak.* He asked his dragon if he knew her. *I do not. But he is most happy with the turn of events. I think him mad with the power of it.*

Danburn pulled his body up and out of the water, taking the towel that Kendrick handed him. She turned just as he moved toward Noah and picked up one of his scales. Without hesitation, she kissed it and then tossed it into the water that he'd only just left. He stood staring at her as the implications of what she'd just done moved over him.

"What?" He shook his head. Now was not the time to tell her that not only had she touched his scale, taking some of the magic from it to her, but other things as well. "Did I do something wrong?"

"On the contrary, what you did was wonderful. I'll explain later. We must see what Noah is upset about."

As soon as he reached them, he knew. He had no idea how he knew that Louisa was the woman that Bullock had, but he listened while he explained what had happened at the police station.

"Four dead, three wounded. The man came in, shot the officer behind the front desk, then shot out all the cameras as he came to them. We have a single blurred picture of him, and I believe it to be Bullock's man, Collier." Noah glanced at him before looking at Kendrick. "He took your sister. As best we can tell, he used chloroform on her and took her out over his shoulder. Then as he left, he turned and shot up the outside cameras before leaving the area. I've taken the liberty of notifying the Feds too. They will be most displeased at the turn of events."

"So we wait now." Danburn didn't like the calmness of Kendrick. When he told her that they'd hear from him soon, knowing that this had to do with the cove, she nodded and smiled at him. "She's going to get her wish, I guess. It was her dream to be the headlines in some paper because someone had taken her. And she told me it would be my fault."

When Kendrick walked away, moving toward the castle, he and Noah both stared after her. When Noah asked him what he should do now, Danburn wanted to tell him that he had no idea, all his energy was focused on Kendrick right now.

*She will be fine. She is stronger than you think.* His dragon chuckled a little. *I would not be surprised if she were to take care of this herself. And when she does, you must let her. If she runs into trouble, we will be beside her to help.*

*She tasted your scale.* He said he was aware of that as well. *We will have a child and he'll be dragon. Do you think she'll mind?*

*I think that whatever happens now is out of our hands. But I must say, I am most happy about it.* So was Danburn, but as his dragon had said, the damage, as it were, was done. *But to think that she did this on her own. Without...she will need to be.... A dragon child. I never thought that...a child of yours and hers will be great.*

As he made his way to follow her, his own step a great deal lighter, he gave little thought to Bullock and Louisa. He was more focused on the babe that would be theirs. A child, their child, would come to them, and he'd be a dragon like him. Moving to the castle, finding her on the steps of their home, he picked her up and held her as she cried. Later, he thought, he'd tell her later what she'd done, when they had Louisa back with them.

~~~

Bernie looked at the woman tied to the chair. He wasn't

really sure if this was the worst idea he'd ever had or the best. But as of yesterday, he was living on the edge. The shipment that had gone out despite the lack of docking had never arrived. He knew that English had everything to do with that. And he was going to pay and pay well for his mistake. Now he was awaiting a call from the man who had been set to receive it.

The woman wasn't as pretty as he'd hoped. She was nice looking, yes, but not pretty. When Collier had brought her to him, he'd thought there had been a mistake. He'd seen pictures of the other woman, the sister, and had thought they'd look some alike. This woman was plain in comparison.

The desperation in his situation had driven him to have Collier go to the jail. He needed things working his way, and having him kill anyone who dared to try and stop him in getting the woman might have been slightly out of proportion to what he had to deal with. But anger had made him rash, and now he had to live with it. Danburn was going to pay for him losing his temper like he had.

As she started to come around, he sat down and tried to have the look of a bored man. He wanted her to think that he did this sort of thing all the time, when in truth, he'd never kidnapped anyone before. Killed, yes. But not simply kidnapped.

"Hello, Louisa. That's your name, isn't it? Louisa Barrera?" She told him it was and told him to let her go. "It doesn't work that way. I make the rules and you will follow them."

"Call my sister and tell her what you want. She'll give it to you. She takes care of me." He asked her about Danburn. "He's not a nice person. I think he's an asshole. Did you know that he has this big castle? They're supposed to send a car for me to take me there, but I think something happened and.... Why am I here, anyway? Are you taking me there? To the castle? I so want to live there."

"As do I." She smiled at him and he thought of sharks. He had no idea why, but that was the first thing that popped into his head. "You're going to call your sister for me and tell her that I have you. Then when she pays up, I'll let you go."

"I'd love to talk to my sister, but your way won't work. The only person I get to talk to is Noah. And he won't give the phone to her no matter what I tell him. And trust me, I have tried and tried until he stopped answering my calls. Even talking to her when I get to see her, she tells me to call him." Bernie frowned as she continued. "I need for you to use softer rope on my wrists. This is cutting into me. And a chair with more cushion. You should also know that I have to pee."

"I'm not going to tie you with silk and give you a more comfortable chair. This is a kidnapping, not an outing with lunch." She asked him what he was serving her for lunch. "I'm not serving you anything until I get what I want."

"You're not very nice. My sister isn't going to like you treating me this way. She takes care of me, and when she finds out what you're doing to me, she is not going to be happy with you." Louisa pulled on the ropes. "When are you going to put softer ropes on me? This is really painful. And the chair, is it coming too?"

Bernie wondered if she was touched in the head. The longer she sat there talking to him, simply ignoring what she didn't want to hear, the more he thought that having her around was going to be more trouble than it was worth. Finally, he told her to shut the fuck up.

"Now, you're going to make a call and tell them that I have you." She asked him again about the ropes. 'There will be no new fucking ropes on you. Mother fuck, are you this stupid?"

"I'm not stupid, but I do have things I want. I'm going to live in the big castle with Kendrick until Danburn tosses her out. Then we're going to have him set up the apartment I was in. It was nice and all, but it wasn't the castle. Plus, there isn't much in the way of furniture anymore. I'll need that taken care of too. When I'm living at the castle, I'm going to be the queen of it." She frowned again. "I don't think they're moving fast enough on my chair and new ropes."

He pulled out his gun and aimed at her. She only stared at him, looking like she knew he wasn't going to shoot her. And the problem was, he needed her too badly to let her get to him. So instead of killing her like he really wanted to do, he left her in the cell. This wasn't going to go well if he couldn't be with her long enough for her to do what he wanted her to.

He saw Collier leaning against the wall across from him. "Get her to make the call." Collier nodded. "She'll drive me crazy before she is done. I've never known a woman so stupid before. I think she might even have Angel beat in that department."

His niece. She was dead, and she did end up in the pit with the others. An accident when Collier had been trying to get her to do what he wanted when he'd met up with her at her apartment. She'd run screaming from him and into traffic before he could stop her. It was either dump her body or have to answer plenty of questions about why she had been tied up when she'd been hit.

Even after questioning Collier about it, Bernie wondered why English had told him to talk to Collier. He was just fine with the way things had turned out with Angel. She was gone, and he didn't have to worry that she'd be around to tell her mom how badly he'd treated her. He supposed having her killed was bad enough, but he couldn't care less right now.

He heard the door open, then close behind him. Good luck was all he could think to say to Collier. He was going to need it. The woman was fucking nuts.

His phone was ringing when he entered his office. Instead of answering it as he had been for the last few days, he let it go to the service. As he was sitting down, he looked out the back of his office into the plant area and smiled.

It had taken him nearly ten years of murdering others and taking over shit territories to get to where he was today. Ten whole years of barely making enough money to afford the smaller things on his want list, much less the bigger ticket items that he really wanted. And now it was within his grasp to not just have his list fulfilled, but to have anything he wanted. If not for the fucker across the way.

When the phone rang again, he turned and looked at the caller ID. The number was blocked, it said. Fine by him. Bernie had made it a habit of never answering those types of calls anyway. Especially after the other day when English had gotten through to him on his cell. Pulling out a pad of paper and making notes on the ransom note that he was going to give English, he revised it to be a demands list about halfway through it. He wasn't really going to give the dumb woman back to English, but he was going to get what he wanted.

His phone rang again five minutes later...same blocked number. He wanted to pick it up. His fingers were itching to do so, but he really didn't want to talk to anyone just yet. But he did turn on the big screen television across from his desk to see what other information they were fumbling with at the crime scene.

Bernie had ordered the shooting, and Collier had claimed that he had to do it the way he had or he would have lost the opportunity to get what Bernie wanted. Besides, he told him, they were able to plant men in the department now that all the good guys had been taken care of. And Collier had assured him that he'd taken care that his face was never seen. Bernie knew that the town was small time, and more than likely only had Internet because it was required of the department to have it. But he'd bet his last nickel that they no more had any way of tracking who had shot up the station than they did the knowledge on how to use anything very high tech. It was why he'd chosen this town for the base of his operation.

When his phone rang again, he picked it up this time. Not saying anything, he listened for several seconds before he heard the sound of a soft laugh. He wasn't sure why, but he had the feeling that he'd made one of the biggest mistakes of his life by answering the call.

"Waiting me out isn't a smart business move, Bernard. I have more important things going on in my life than waiting for some shit to answer his phone, then when he does, waiting for him to speak." Bernie swallowed twice, trying to get his vocal cords to work with his now thickening tongue. "When are you getting my goods to me? I have a long list of clients that are just chomping at the bit to have a taste of what I was supposed to receive from you several days ago. I do not care for waiting. On calls to be answered, nor the things that I want."

"I'm working on it right now. The men, they're working round the clock to make sure that we have the entire order ready for you as planned." Michael Hollywood laughed. "There shouldn't be any trouble this time around. You'll have everything that I promised you in this shipment."

"No, there had better not be. As for my completed order, I'm not sure you understand how this works. When I place an order, I expect it to come. When it does not, through no fault of my own, you're supposed to double my order. At no extra charge to me, of course." The laughter again. "You should be a man that is true to his word, Bernard. However will you make it in this world if you are doubted at every turn?"

Double? Christ, they were going to be cutting it close now. Even with working the men twenty hours a day. He asked if he could have an extension.

"Why, of course. But the same penalties apply. You don't have my order, the full order when it's due, then I get to have double that. For no extra charge again." The soft laughter again. This time it was chilling, and bringing sweat to his brow at the same time. "I am a man who does not like to be trifled with. And you have taken my patience with you to the limit, Bernard."

No one but his mother had ever called him by his given name. Bernie had not allowed it after she passed. Now this man was using it as if he had a right to, and there wasn't shit he could do about it. Collier walked in, looking pissed off when Bernie spoke to Mr. Hollywood.

"Sir, I'm sure you can understand the issues that I'm having here. The people here, they might be hard up for some income, but they have no concept of how this works. It's all I can do to keep a good crew working for me without them fucking up my—"

"Profanity is not necessary, Bernard. Please. Let us be civil about this. But as you were saying, you have poor workers. Then I would suggest that you rid yourself of the dead weight and move on." The sound of papers being shuffled came over the phone line, and Bernie closed his eyes, afraid of what Hollywood was going to say next. "I'm a generous man, so I will tell you what I'm going to do. I have some men, good workers, who will gladly come and work on my order with you. And once you are caught up, you know, with all of your orders to me, then they will return to me. How does that sound?"

"And what will this generosity cost me?" The laughter again, and Bernie thought it got more and more scary all the time. "Not that I don't think you have some good reliable workers, but I should know up front what I'm going to be dealing with."

"Yes, smart on your part. It will only cost you a part of your business. I think a sixty-forty cut should cover my expenses and the wait I have to endure." Bernie asked him how the cut would work. "Oh, you would get the lesser, of course. I do have to send my men to you. Then there is the added expense of their payroll. You can pay that to them weekly, as you are your own men. Then I will expect a percentage of their income too. Not from their checks, but you covering it for them. It wouldn't be fair of us to charge them for your incompetence, now would it?"

"No. But I don't think I can afford that, Mr. Hollywood. As I said, I'm cutting it close to the margin now." Mr. Hollywood told him he didn't understand. It only took Bernie about two seconds to realize that it was going to be his way or else.

"The men will arrive in about three hours. And when they get there, I will expect you to let me know that they have arrived safely. The first check you send me...well, not a check. You'll send me cash. But the first installment will be given to me twenty-four hours after they arrive. Then every week until we have finished our business. The checks, as it were, will be given directly to me; that way I can be assured of getting my end of our little deal."

After a few more minutes of Bernie being told how things were going to work, the call ended. He didn't say a word as he thought of what had just happened to him and his little business. When Collier said his name, probably not for the first time, he told him what had just transpired between him and his now new partner in this.

"How the hell are you going to afford that?" He told him he had no idea other than to pay it and not die. "Christ, he's going to be making more than you are at this, and you're still going to be doing all the work on your own."

He knew that. But as far as he could see, there wasn't any way out of it. When Hollywood spoke, people usually listened or ended up dead. He wasn't ready to call the undertakers just yet. Bernie decided to change the subject, just to get his mind off the new deals he had been forced into.

"The woman, did she make the call?" When Collier scrubbed his hand over his face, Bernie had to smile. The few minutes that he'd spent with her had been bad enough. Collier had been with her for over an hour. "I take it there weren't any calls made."

"Oh, she gave me the number all right. Even told me who to ask for when it started ringing. But as soon as I put the phone to her ear for her to tell them what I wanted, she started talking about the castle and how she was going to need a much nicer room after all of this. And that we won't give her any kind of nicer chair and silk bonds. I have no fucking clue what she's talking about with that shit."

Bernie explained. "So we're not closer to having what we want than before." Collier said he would go back down in a moment, that he just needed a break. "I'd just make her scream in to the phone, then tell them what we need for them to get her back. No more fucking around. The faster we can get this mess cleaned up, the faster I can get rid of Hollywood's men and I can move on to more important matters, like making me money."

Once he had what he wanted from English, he was going to simply walk away from this business. He'd thought of that while talking to Hollywood. The man would take over anyway. Why should he hang around only to have himself killed when this deal was done and he was no longer of use to him? Selling the woman back to English, or the illusion of selling her back, would net him enough money that he'd be able to set up again. Just not in this area.

When Collier got up to leave, Bernie went with him. He wasn't in the best of moods, so he thought he'd go and take a little of his frustrations out on the woman. She was going to die anyway. He might as well have a little fun with her now. As soon as he entered the room, she started on about the nicer chair that had not arrived and the silk bonds. He wished to Christ now he'd never used that word.

"You'll do as you're told, or so help me, I'm going to blow your fucking brains out." She just stared at him. Collier must have hit her earlier, because her lip was puffy. When she opened her mouth, he warned her again. "If you so much as mention the chair or the ropes holding you, I will do it."

"My sister won't be happy with you treating me this way." He asked her how she'd feel if he was to kill her. "It would devastate her. I'm her sister after all. I'll ask her, but I think that you're being terribly mean to me."

"Yeah, I think you'll get over it." Collier put the phone to her mouth, leaving it on speakerphone so they could hear what was being said on both ends. As soon as the phone was answered, the man's voice at the other end sounding bored, Bernie hit Louisa across the mouth and sent her flying to the floor. As she lay there screaming at him, he took the phone from Collier.

"You want her back? You have Danburn meet me at the lake in twenty minutes. Tell him I'm done fucking around and I want him to pay up." The man said he would give him the message. "If I see cops, I'm going to kill the woman and Danburn. I'm sure you know what sort of man I am."

"Yes, I understand what sort of man you think you are. Big and bad. But you have no idea what sort of person you are threatening when you speak of his lordship this way." Bernie told him to do what he was told. "Yes, I will, but I have a message for you as well."

When there was nothing forthcoming, Bernie thought he'd hung up. But when the woman spoke, the cultured voice of someone that had taken the phone from the man who had answered, Bernie thought of Hollywood and his soft voice over the phone.

"My name is Kendrick Barrera. If you hurt my sister, you piece of shit, I will come after you and you will rue the day that you messed with what is mine." He asked her about Danburn. "Him? I'm not worried about him. He's going to stomp you into the ground so far that no one will find you for centuries. If the earth even takes you inside of it."

"What?" She only laughed, a laugh that made his skin crawl and his balls tighten up around his throat, it felt like. "You'd better watch your step, Miss Barrera. I have something of yours."

"I'm not afraid of you either. And I swear to you, if she's hurt, you're going to pay." The line went dead and he looked at Collier. The man was pale, and he wondered about that until Louisa started laughing.

"I told you. I told you that she was going to hurt you for this. Didn't I tell you? Now, what about that chair? Where is my chair?" Bernie wasn't sure he could take too much more, and before he could think he should walk away, he pulled his gun out and shot her in the head. He looked at Collier when he spoke.

"That's not going to be helpful. Christ, what the fuck have you done now? I know, I think you just fucked us all over. And I for one am not going to be the fall guy in this shit."

Bernie shot him too. When he realized what he'd done, killed two people that he needed more than he could think right now, Bernie sat down on the floor and contemplated putting a bullet in his own head. He had no idea what he had to do now, but went to his office to gather up more ammo and guns. Time to clean house.

# *Chapter 12*

Danburn was going to go out there, kill the man, then move on. He was sick to death of this monster ruining his life...had been since he'd moved in next door. It was only recently that the earth had told him what all was going on, and that she was upset by the death and destruction of her body the earth. She'd said that men were making something that clogged up not just her earth, but the air that they needed as well. Meth, he'd told her. They were making drugs to sell.

*You will do well to be careful.* The dragon, his dragon, was speaking to him more and more. As he made his way to the lake, he continued with his warnings. *I cannot safely say that I will not help you should he —*

He felt it, the movement in the earth. As Danburn stood there, his body swaying slightly, he felt the earth screaming in pain. He started to ask what had happened when his dragon spoke to him again.

*I'm so sorry, Danburn. She is no more. Her body has been*

*tossed with the others that have died senselessly.* Danburn held onto the tree next to him. He could feel its pain too. The death of anyone hurt them some, but when it was his family, it hurt them more. When his father had died, the earth mourned as they did, for months without stop.

*How? How did she die?* Dragon told him, telling him that with her death there was another. A man that was also with her in death. *In the pit? The one you were telling me about? She's been put there?*

*Yes. There are nine bodies there. The earth feels them like they are beneath her soil, but they are only atop it. Their blood stains her badly.*

Danburn reached down, digging his fingers into the soil and telling her how profoundly sorry he was. *I will rid the world of him today. He will no longer be able to take and take without consequences.*

*Thank you, my lord dragon. The death of my lady's sister, it will be hard for her to accept.* Danburn thought perhaps that Kendrick had already figured that Louisa would never survive this. Not that she would want her dead, but Louisa wasn't going to cooperate if the first phone call was any indication. *We will take her within us. Give life to the earth around her so that our lady will be able to know that we are sorrowful for her loss.*

Danburn thanked her and stood up. His dragon, the beast within him, stretched and seemed to curl around him. Good. If the shit hit the fan, as he knew it was going to, he wanted to know that he was there for him. Turning when he heard his name, he was both happy and upset that Kendrick had joined him.

"She's gone. I just heard from...well, the earth told me." He nodded. "That horrible man killed her for no reason other than she was my sister and he wanted something from us. I want him to suffer. I want him to know that to fuck with my family is to fuck with the wrong person."

"I'm going to take care of him." She shook her head and moved ahead of him. He might have told her to turn back, that he would make sure that Bullock and Collier paid, but he paused. Whatever happened, she needed to be as much a part of it as he was. As she said, family was being messed with, and he was going to make sure that Bullock knew it.

The lake was peaceful, the time that they'd spent there yesterday now forgotten with the violence of the day. He wanted to go there as his dragon, burn all of Bullock's existence from this earth, but he was working with some people who might not understand if he were to suddenly become a dragon and burn the man to the ground.

Before he could clear the line of trees, he saw Kendrick talking to Bullock, his gun pointed right at her. Danburn started to shout for her to run, but his dragon told him to let him go. Before he could try and figure out his intentions, Danburn felt his body being consumed and he stood there not as a man, but as his large beast.

*He will not see us until it is too late. The others, they will not know any different than we let them see.* He asked him what he meant, what kind of trickery that the dragon was going to pull. *Our body is one with that which is around us. The earth, she holds us firmly, and we will not falter in this fight.*

*The police are nearby. They're not going to believe that Bullock just died, no matter how you think we can kill him.* His beast asked him to trust him. *I do. With all that I am. But our mate is there, alone, with a gun on her.*

They moved forward. Danburn liked to think he had some part in their movement, but he knew as well as the dragon did that the only reason he was there was that there

179

had been no choice in the matter. As soon as they were within touching distance of Kendrick, the dragon lay down. Even when Bullock looked in their direction, Danburn knew that he couldn't see him.

*You cannot move fast enough if he tries to hurt her.* His beast told him to listen to them. *I need her safe.*

*As do I, but you must listen to them.* He looked at the couple in front of him. *Kendrick, she is most brave.*

She was yelling at him. Not really yelling, he supposed, but more that she was scolding him. Her voice was calm, but her demeanor was that of one who was sorely disappointed in whomever they were speaking to. He watched her carefully and felt the dragon move again. His hand was snaking across the grass toward her. He knew then that she'd be safe should Bullock try to shoot at her.

"You don't know shit. Where is that boyfriend of yours? English? I want to talk to him about what is going on. And if you want to see that sister of yours again, you'll keep your mouth shut. Unless, of course, you want to put it around my cock." Danburn felt the low growl rumble from the dragon's belly. He told him to be steady, that she was fine. Both Kendrick and Bullock looked in their direction. "What the fuck was that?"

"Dogs. You don't have Louisa. Not anymore anyway, do you? You killed her and threw her in a pit behind the manufacturing building that you put up." Bullock raised his gun up and Kendrick slapped it away. "You're not going to shoot me, you fucking idiot. I'm going to find out why you did what you did to Louisa."

"Sure she's dead. A lot of people are. But Christ almighty, have you ever talked to her?" Danburn had to smile. Yes, he had, and he could understand the frustration, but not to the point of killing her. "She was a fucking idiot. A parrot that kept saying the same thing over. Where is my chair? Where are the silk ropes? My sister does this. My sister will do that. I just couldn't take it anymore."

As he bent to pick up the gun, Kendrick turned and winked at Danburn. She could see him. He had no idea how she could. His camouflage was nearly perfect, but she had looked right at him. Danburn started to ask Dragon when Bullock pointed the gun at her again.

"You killed her because she annoyed you. You killed my sister because she annoyed you, and then you threw her in that hole that you've put others in like she was nothing more than the trash." Bullock said that he'd done her a favor, and she should be grateful to him. "Grateful? You fucking prick. I hate you."

The slap, Danburn knew from experience, was painful. But on a human, it would be more so. When Bullock landed on the ground, Dragon made his move. Kendrick didn't so much as scream when Bullock was suddenly crushed to death when Dragon's head smashed him into the lawn.

~~~

Kendrick didn't look in the direction of the house. She knew that Danburn was coming for her, but she was a little nervous as to how he would arrive. The big dragon didn't scare her, not at all, but she'd seen what he'd done to Mr. Bullock and it made her a little nauseous to think about it. Strong arms wrapped around her from behind, and Kendrick felt the tears fall that she'd been barely holding onto. When Officer Ludlow cleared his throat, she looked at him.

"I don't know what happened to him. We were talking and all of the sudden he was...that rock just smashed on top of him. I only slapped him, but I didn't have anything to do with that rock falling." She turned her head toward where a blanket lay over the body. It was concave now and covered in a deep rust color, the large stone laying nearby, blood covering one side where they had moved it off the body. "Do you think we can talk over there? Near the trees?"

"Yes. I'm so sorry." Jake moved to stand behind her so that when she turned to look at him, her back was to the bloodied body of the monster who had murdered so many. "When he admitted to killing your sister, we made moves to come and take him into our custody. There was...we're still thinking it was a small earth tremor, but there was movement under our feet and for several seconds, we weren't looking at you. I'm not saying you did this. I'm not sure what did it, but you couldn't have.... What I mean is, you weren't strong enough to have caused.... We know that you are innocent of his death."

There was a boulder or stone, whatever they were calling it, there now. It hadn't been there when Bernie had been crushed, but added afterwards. Kendrick was glad that he was dead, more than she was letting the police know. But to see him die, that wasn't anything she wanted to see with anyone ever again.

"They're looking for your sister and another man by the name of David Collier. We've had a tip of a burial site just behind a building, but so far we're dealing with the labs that we found there too. As soon as we find her, Miss Barrera, we'll let you know." She nodded, knowing these men and women had more important things to consider than a woman who may or may not be dead.

When Jake walked away, she turned in Danburn's arms and let him hold her. "He spoke to me, your dragon." Danburn lifted her chin up, and she looked into his eyes when he asked her what he'd said. "He told me to close my eyes and not to open them until he told me. But I was too afraid. Tell him that

I'm sorry."

"He said to tell you that he loves you." She laid her head back on his chest and was soothed by the beating of his heart. "Are you all right, love? Do you want to go home now?"

"Yes. Home. I want to go home." He pulled her into his arms again, this time with him beside her. "I love you, Danburn. Very much, but I don't think I'm up for that thing tonight. What if we just skipped it? I'm sure that they'll understand. Won't they?"

She nearly fell over when he suddenly stopped. "Say it again. I want to see your face when you tell me again."

"I love you. And the beast inside of you. I love you both with all of my heart." He picked her up this time and swung her around in a circle. Laughing when he sat her down, she held him to her as he kissed her. She could feel his love as if he were soaking her in it.

"I love you as well. With all that we are, both he and I will cherish you for the rest of our days together." Danburn went down on one knee and kissed the ring on her finger the earth had given her so short a time ago. "Will you marry me? Will you...? I have to tell you something. The kiss you bestowed on my scale. You made it so that when we have a child, it will be dragon. As pure as if he were born to you as a dragon."

"Dragon told me." She put her hand over her belly and looked at Danburn as he stayed bent on his knee. "I want a child with you. Lots of children. I want them soon."

"We can do that." She grinned at him. "I was closing up the castle when I met you. Would you...would you live here with me and my mom? Raise our children here instead of in town?"

"I would like nothing better." When he stood up, she went to his open arms without hesitation. "Soon, Danburn. I really do want to have children soon."

When he started to the woods, she kissed his neck. As she got closer to the darkness of the trees, Kendrick had his shirt undone, his buttons scattering as he walked. By the time they were ten yards into the woods where no one could see them, he had her pressed against a tree and was pulling off her blouse.

"You wear entirely too many clothes when we're together." She wanted to answer him, to tell him that society demanded that she was at least partly clothed, when he dropped to his knees in front of her. "I'm going to feast on you. Drink every drop of your cream before I take you here, right here in our forest."

"Yes. Please hurry." Her pants were ripped from her. She might have mourned their quick death, but Danburn had his mouth on her pussy and was sliding his finger deep inside of her as he lapped at her clit. Her first climax nearly took her breath away, but he didn't stop when she came three more times.

His free hand was moving over her, pinching at her nipple, tugging at her breast. Even when she thought him finished with her, her releases nearly crippling her, he touched her, suckled at her everywhere he could reach.

"Please. I need you." He only sucked harder on her clit, bringing her again and again as she held onto him and the branches above her. "Danburn, I can't stand up any more. I need to— Oh, yes."

He stood, turned her around, and was deep inside of her before she could finish her begging. He fucked her hard as she bent almost double. His fingers never slowed as they tormented her pussy. Even as she screamed out she was coming, he lifted her up, his cock still deep in her, and squeezed her breast hard, bringing her once again.

"Come again." He nuzzled her neck as he commanded her. "Come for us. We'll fill you with our child."

Reaching blindly for something to hold on to, her fingers brushed over the tree in front of her. Holding on to it, she felt his teeth graze over her flesh. And when he sank them into her, tearing into her flesh, Kendrick screamed around the pain and the pleasure as the darkness swallowed her up.

When she woke, Kendrick was laying in their bed alone. The room was bright with sunlight and there wasn't any sound coming from anywhere in the room. Sitting up, she saw the flowers first, then the note. Getting up slowly, just realizing how sore she was, Kendrick smelled the fragrant roses and then opened the note.

*"I've had to go into town today. I'm so sorry to leave you right now, but I'll be back around noon. Or at least that's the time I'm shooting for."* Sitting down, she finished the note. *"Noah is taking care of the calls for you. Should you need anything, the staff will make sure you have it. Please don't answer the phone."*

It occurred to her then…her sister was dead. A man that had been crushed to death by a large dragon had killed her, too. Kendrick felt the sorrow of Louisa's death move over her in waves. It wasn't until a voice—the dragon, he told her—spoke that she realized she'd been thinking of joining Louisa. Kendrick felt guilty for not taking better care of her when she was alive.

*You should not think those thoughts.* She asked him why. *Because we need you. Both Danburn and I, we love you very much and need you with us.*

*I should have done more to keep her safe.* He told her that she could only do so much before she had to stand back. *And let her learn on her own? I'm pretty sure that the only thing that Louisa*

185

*learned in all her life was how to get what she wanted.*

*She wasn't one that went without. Even at the cost of others' happiness. I know that you loved her very much. It is only natural that she has left you feeling lost.* She told him that her heart hurt. *Yes. I'm sure that it does. I know the feelings that you are having now. They are overwhelming and sometimes leave you to feel that you cannot go on. But you must, for Danburn and myself.*

*Who did you lose? I thought that you were only a part of Danburn. I'm sorry. I didn't mean to be crass.* He told her that she was not. *Who left a hole in your heart?*

*When Danburn's father was alive — he was called Fletcher, by the way — his dragon and I, like father and son, were the same. His dragon was my sire. His mother's dragon is my mother. When you have children, it will be the same relationship as you have with the human part of them.* She sat up in her chair, loving the idea that the dragons, even though they were a part of them, had family too. *And though you will remain a human — we cannot change someone — you will be the mother of the sons and daughters you have, as well as the dragons that are a part of them.*

*Danburn and you both told me that because I touched your scale to my mouth, my children will be full-blooded dragons. I don't know how that will work. I mean...will I have babies or eggs? Your kind have eggs, correct?* She felt his laughter and wasn't embarrassed by it. *You laugh like Danburn. Full of life.*

*Because I am. And no, you will have babies, just as you should. Their dragon will be born when they have reached a certain age. In human years that will be only ten years. Their dragon will be with them, guiding them on the right paths, telling them what they will need to learn to be a good man and dragon, but they will not shift into one until their body is mature enough to take our size. And so that you will not have to care for a large dragon as a babe.* He laughed again. *We are quite large, even as small children.*

She got up to go to the bathroom and get her shower. *Why is it that you can talk to me? I love it, but I don't understand why you can talk to me, and I'm assuming that Danburn cannot hear.*

*Because you are my mate as well. I can speak with you both at the same time, should you wish it. But I am as much your mate as Danburn is, so it is only reasonable that we can talk.* Kendrick turned on the water and thought perhaps there was more to it than that. *There is, my lady. You have given me your blood freely. We are one, you and I, as Danburn and I are.*

After she showered and dressed, Kendrick made her way to the lower levels of the castle. Smiling, she thought of the fact that she lived with a dragon in a castle. It was almost too fairy tale like to be real. But as she made her way through the living room and to the kitchen, she paused when she saw the paintings on the walls, as well as the many sculptures that were on stands and pedestals. She turned to Noah when he entered the room with her.

"That is Danburn the fourth. The blue one next to him is his son, the fifth. Each generation is here, including Danburn's father. See?" She looked at the dragon painted there and stepped closer to it. "He was a fierce dragon. A good and kind man, but his dragon was untamed at times. I sometimes think that he died sadly. An infection befell him, when he so wished to die on the battlefield."

Kendrick ran her fingers over the scales of the painting. They were almost real; the artist had done a wonderful job of capturing not just his body, but his eyes seemed to look right at her. When her fingers touched the wings, spread wide and tattered from his battles, she saw the signature in the corner of the painting. She turned to Noah.

"You did this." He nodded and moved to the other paintings, ones as old as this castle, she'd bet. His name was on them all. "You did them all. You painted them.... You were alive with each of them?"

"I was their keeper. Each male dragon born to the family, I moved to care for them." He bowed low and smiled at her when he rose up. "And when you have a child, a boy dragon, I will move to care for him, never leaving the household here, but taking care of the man he becomes."

"I thought you were.... I guess I just thought you were like me. A human that came to be a part of a dragon's family." He told her no, he was the keeper. "So you have been.... Wow, you've been around for a lot longer than I thought."

"I have been around for a lot longer than anyone thinks. And I should like to keep it that way, if you please." She nodded. "Someday I shall paint you, and you will hang with the other lady dragons and their mates."

"But I'm not a dragon. I'll look sort of out of place, don't you think?" He nodded down the hall, one that she'd only just noticed, and she followed him. "Oh Noah, this is beautiful."

"It's called the family hall. Soon after the house was made, I asked Danburn for a room. One to put all my paintings in and a room I could paint in. Several days later, he brought me to this hall and told me to hang them here. There was no hall here when the castle was built."

She moved down the hall, looking at the pairs of dragons as they stood side by side. Generations of them, from the beginning of time until she got to Elissa and Fletcher. In all the portraits, there was only one human.

"She was a woman of worth, Lady Paige was. She bore her mate only one child, but he was a great man, like his sire." Kendrick stared at the dragon that stood over his mate as Lady Paige sat upon his hand. She had on a dress of chainmail, Kendrick noticed, and a sword in her hand as she smiled at them. "When her mate was killed during a siege on their castle, she lay beside him, her heart broken, and died as well. Their love was that which romance is based on, I believe."

"She looks like she could conquer worlds if she had to." Noah said that they had. "I would like to be like her. Strong and dependable."

"But, my lady, you are much like her." She turned to look at him, shaking her head. "You are. You vanquished the man who would harm this family without thought to what it would do to you. You avenged your sister's death by confronting the man who killed her. You saved this family, all of us, when you stood in front of the murderer and never backed away."

"The dragon killed him." Noah said that the dragon was only the instrument. She was the one that wielded the power so that it could happen. "I'm not brave. I'm afraid of my own shadow."

"You are stronger than you think. And as for your shadow, you should see it the way we do." Kendrick asked him what he meant. Instead of answering her, he took her to the small slit of a window and stood her in front of it. "Look at it. Your shadow."

It took her a moment to see it. But there she was, a dragon that seemed to grow from her feet and stretch out from there to the wall in front of her. And as Kendrick watched, her dragon spread her wings wide, showing her that she was there for her and that they were one. Kendrick felt the tears prickle at her eyes when she realized that she wasn't helpless at all.

"She's mine." Noah nodded and took her back to the painting of Lady Paige. There he showed her the shadow that stood so proudly in front of that woman too. "Oh Noah, thank you so very much."

"It is my pleasure, my lady."

# Chapter 13

Danburn was in his office when he heard a woman speaking in a loud screeching voice. Getting up to see what was going on, he was surprised to see Julia there. The two men with her were holding her back, but it was obvious to him that she'd meant to harm Connie.

"What's the meaning of this?" No one moved, and Julia stopped yelling to look at him. "I thought you were in jail. Why are you here harassing my staff?"

"I wanted to talk to you." Danburn leaned against the doorjamb. "Not out here. Somewhere private. Where we can be uninterrupted."

"I don't think so. Whatever you have to say to me, you can say it here or not at all." She actually stomped her foot. "What is it that you think you have to say to me, Julia? I have a lot of work to do before I go home to my wife."

It felt good saying that. It wasn't actually true as yet; tomorrow they were going to have a short ceremony at the castle, and a few guests, mostly staff, were going to celebrate with them.

Danburn looked over at Jake when he laughed. "You have something funny you'd like to share with me?" Julia looked terrible, and when she turned on Jake, Danburn realized that he was a lucky man that he'd found out what she was before it was too late. "I don't think anything about this situation is the least bit funny."

"Really? Because I do." Jake looked at him as he continued. "She thinks to come here and tell you that she's going to have your kid, when we all know that's not even close to being the truth. The doc confirmed it as a lie a few days ago. And I think she wants you to drop everything and bail her out. Something about you two being best friends. Are you, Danburn, her bestie?"

"No." Julia stomped her foot again when he answered Jake. "Okay, so that's taken care of. You're lying, as usual, and I'm not going to bail you out of anything. What you did, you did all on your own."

"He made me do it." Danburn couldn't help it, he burst out laughing. "Well, he did. He said that once I got you where we wanted you, then I could have you. What could I have done under the circumstances? I love you, Danburn."

"So do I." Everyone turned and looked at Kendrick when she emerged from the elevator. She looked amazingly beautiful, and he put out his hand for her to come to him. Instead, she moved in front of Julia, and he watched as Jake and the man with him backed up. Jake held onto Julia, but not as tightly as he had been, Danburn noticed. "What do you think you're doing here? Poaching? I'll have you know that I'm very protective of Danburn, and I'd really hate to have to hurt you."

"Hurt me? You think you can hurt me any more than he has by claiming there was nothing between us? Did he tell you about me? About all the nights that we spent together in bed, fucking like animals?" Danburn started to speak, but Connie put her hand on his arm to stay him. "We were meant for each other, him and me. And he'll soon regret not taking me when he had the chance."

"I'm sure that will never cross his mind. But as for you being an animal? Yes, he told me about you. How you were greedy in bed. Never seeing to his needs. What sort of woman does that to her lover?" Kendrick looked Julia up and down and nodded. "Okay, I guess that answers my question. You're a bitch."

"Why, you fucking cunt." As Julia struggled to get at Kendrick, Jake winked at Danburn as he let her go. As Danburn took a step toward the two women, Julia knocked her body into Kendrick. Never missing a single beat, Kendrick drew back her fist and hit Julia right in the face. Blood poured from her nose as she fell back on the floor. You hit me. You fucking, bitch, you hit me."

"Yes, and if you get up, I will gladly do it again." Kendrick actually put out her hand to help her up, and Julia didn't take it. "Well, that's too bad. I was really looking forward to knocking you on your fat ass again."

As she was led away, screaming about suing Kendrick, Danburn took his love in his arms. He felt her shaking and thought she was crying, but when he looked into her face, he could see tears, but they were from laughter, not sadness.

"You are a violent little thing, aren't you?" She grinned and nodded. "I guess I'll have to remember you have a hell of a right hook. Christ, that was amazing."

"It felt good too." He took her into his office and closed the door behind them. When she sat at his desk, Danburn waited by the door. He knew that there had to be a reason for her to just show up like this.

Her sister's funeral was yesterday. They had buried her in the family plot and given her a lovely stone to mark her passing. Danburn also knew that Kendrick had gone to the attorney's office earlier today, filling out the paperwork to claim part of the money that had been found at the Bullock massacre.

All the men and women who had worked there had been murdered and left in the building before Bullock had come to the lake to kill him. Even the women who worked in the kitchens had been shot dead where they had stood working.

"They're saying that any claims made at the Bullock estate will be divided up between the families of the victims. I know that we can afford to have her buried and everything, but I applied anyway. I want to use the money to start a scholarship fund for the local high school in Louisa's name. The attorney said that it might only be about five thousand dollars, but that'll help someone, don't you think?" He told her they would add to it every year too. She moved around the room, picking up items and then putting them back in the same place. When she got to the window, he asked her what else had happened. "Nothing really. I just thought I'd come to see you, see if you wanted to have lunch with me. Then she was here."

"She's gone now, and I'm free for lunch." Even if he wasn't, he'd clear his calendar for the week if she wanted him to. "I have to go to the food pantry for about an hour after lunch. I'd be honored if you were to go with me."

"How much do you donate to the local charities?" The question caught him off guard, and he had to think. "The reason I ask is, one of the families at the lawyer's office handling the money looked like they could use a hand up. I mean, like a handful of hands up. Their son was one of the dead. He'd been sending home a few dollars a week when he was paid to help his parents raise his children. I want to...how do you go about having a fundraiser around here? On a large scale?"

"My mom would know. She's done it in the past. Not on a huge scale, but she had a fundraiser about four years ago to help fill the pantry for the holidays." She nodded but didn't say anything more. "I'm sure that she'd help you get it started."

"I want to raise money for two different groups, if that's possible. Mental illness and depression. I was thinking that would cover a lot of people. Give some hope where they might not think there is any." He nodded. "Then I want to raise money to help with the pantry, now that you mention it, and gifts for children."

"Those are very good causes, love." She nodded. "Kendrick, tell me what happened today...besides the family you met. You were in such a wonderful mood when you left the house."

"Did you know that there used to be a homeless shelter in town? It's been closed for nearly ten years, I guess. I stayed there one time when I was in a bad way, and Louisa, she... well, I couldn't go back. But it served food once a day to as many as there was food for, and they gave out blankets and coats when they had them. The funding was hard to come by, I guess, and doctors decided that it really wasn't worth their time to go there and help either. After a while, people stopped helping and it had to close up." He moved toward her, sitting in the chair across from his desk as she continued. "Pierce said he'd help me get it going with the doctors again.

He also knows of a lot of grants and low interest loans we can get to help get it going. He said that he'd work there when he wasn't needed at the estate, and that he was sure there were others that would help out as well."

"I'll give you the money." She told him that she didn't want that. She wanted to do this on her own. "Okay, but we can donate what you don't get from the rest."

"Thank you. I'll need to figure this out, but I don't want to sit around and wait for you to come home. I want to have something that I can call my own. Even if I never get paid for it in money." He was so proud of her that he wanted to pick her up in his arms and hold her. "I want this to mean something to more than just those we help. I want the community to be a large part of it too."

Danburn had no idea what had made her start thinking in this direction until Dragon spoke to him. *A man down on his luck asked her for her change, and she had none. Not even a dollar, and she felt badly about it. Instead of walking away, she took him to the deli around the corner and tried to buy him something to eat. They turned him away because of what he was. She was so furious at the woman at the counter, she called Noah and had him look into buying the place so she could fire her.* He asked Dragon what the man was. *Homeless, my lord. Nothing more than a man down on his luck.*

"When do you want to start this? We have two buildings in the downtown area that would be perfect for this. One of them was a former hotel." She turned and looked at him, and he could see she really wanted this. "We can start the work on them to bring them up to code today if you want."

"I do." He nodded and reached for his phone. "I might have purchased a restaurant too, just so you know. I'd like to... there is this woman there that I want to fire. Or I did. But now

I want her to work there if we get it, and serve all the homeless that come in as a sort of penance." He laughed as the phone rang at his ear. "I guess you heard about it."

"A little." He told her that he loved her. "And you should know that if you want it, then it's yours. I love the way your mind works."

Two hours later not only did they have a crew of men going to start on cleaning up the hotel, but he had two people interested in helping run it. His staff, it seemed, liked the idea as much as he did. As he was headed to the door to take his lovely future wife to lunch, Connie stopped him.

"There is a young woman in the lobby that is in need of a place to stay." He asked her what was going on. "She's like you, sir. A lady dragon."

He nodded. It wasn't the first time that he'd been approached by another of his kind, but now he wanted to help instead of sending them on their way. But before he could tell her to set up an appointment with her, Kendrick spoke up.

"Find out if she can organize and help me. I'm going to need myself a Noah before this is all done." Connie smiled and said she'd find out. "Good. And find her a place to stay as well, please, and whatever else she might require while we figure out what to do with her."

As they went down in the elevator, he pulled Kendrick into his arms and kissed her. She asked him what it was for, so he kissed her again.

"You keep that up and we'll never make it to lunch." He said that was fine by him. "No, I'm starved, and you owe me for making me late for breakfast this morning."

"Yes, but you scream out your releases so prettily. I can't help it if you're so delicious." She smacked him on the chest. "I love you, Kendrick."

"And I love you, but you're still taking me to lunch, buster. I've had an eventful morning." If he had his way, she'd have a more eventful evening.

**Before You Go...**

# HELP AN AUTHOR

## *write a review*

# THANK YOU!

Share your voice and help guide other readers to these wonderful books. Even if it's only a line or two your reviews help readers discover the author's books so they can continue creating stories that you'll love. Login to your favorite retailer and leave a review. Thank you.

Kathi Barton, author of the bestselling series Force of Nature, lives in Nashport, Ohio with her husband Paul. In addition to writing full time Kathi likes to spend time with her eight grandkids, three children and three children-in-laws. She writes to relax and have fun.

Her muse, a cross between Jimmy Stewart and Hugh Jackman brings them to life for her readers in a way that has them coming back time and again for more. Her favorite genre is paranormal romance with a great deal of spice. You can visit Kathi on line and drop her an email if you'd like. She loves hearing from her fans. aaronskiss@gmail.com.

Follow Kathi on her blog: http://kathisbartonauthor.blogspot.com/